THE CONFECTIONER'S EXILE

CLAIRE LUANA

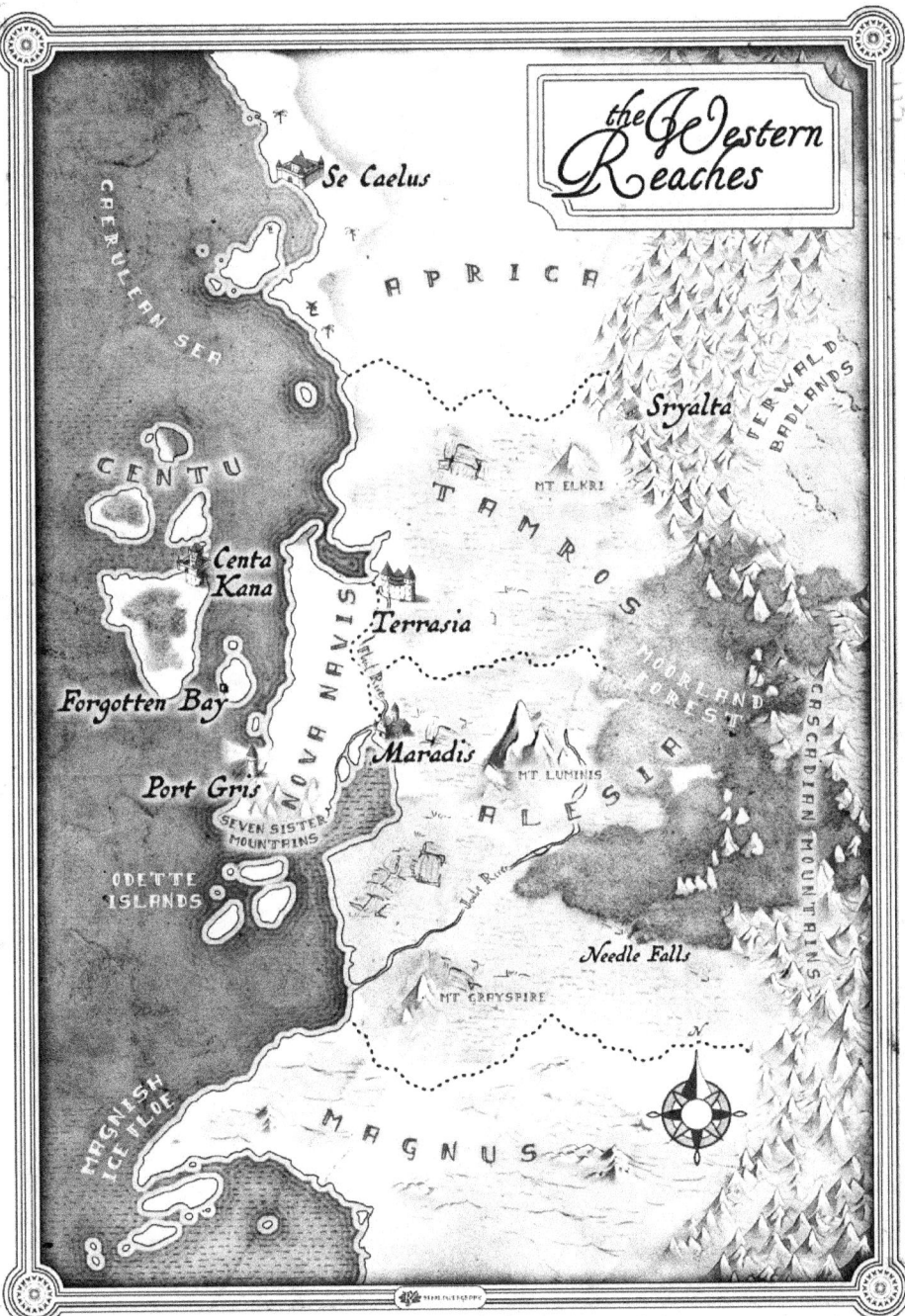

CHAPTER 1

The afternoon sun gleamed off the horse's sweat-lathered flanks. The racetrack's crowd roared as the ebony beast rounded the corner, pulling ahead of the dappled stallion next to him.

Hale's friend Roan leaned forward from their viewing box, roaring for the stallion to run.

Hale grinned in satisfaction. The little black horse would win this race—Hale could feel it. And the victory would be all the sweeter knowing that the long odds on the horse would net him a pretty penny.

Roan's groans were echoed throughout the stadium as the black horse crossed the finish line two noses ahead of the gray stallion. Roan collapsed back in his wicker chair with an expression of such despair that Hale couldn't help but chuckle.

"Did you bet on the black?" Hale's brother, Calladan, leaned forward, squinting suspiciously at Hale.

A wide grin stretched across Hale's tan face.

"Of course you did." Cal rolled his eyes. "Because when do things *not* go your way?"

"It's not my fault I like an underdog," Hale said.

"Yet somehow you always pick the right underdog," Roan said. "When I play the long odds I always lose my shirt."

Hale picked at his friend's seersucker button-down playfully. "You could stand to lose this shirt. No one is wearing salmon this season."

"I didn't know it was possible, but you grow more insufferable by the day," Cal quipped.

"You took the words right out of my mouth," Roan said.

"Yet you keep coming back for more." Hale ruffled Roan's and Cal's blond heads as they both struggled to escape his grasp.

"I'm stuck with you, brother," Cal said. "I'm not sure what his excuse is."

"I'm here for Hale's castoff ladies," Roan said, draining the copper mug set before him, the sweat from the mug leaving a ring of condensation on the glass table. "Consoling them after their inevitable heartbreak has become almost a full-time job for me."

"Now, mates, green's not a good color on either of you. I'm very open with my admirers. They know what they're getting with me and they know what they're not. It's not my fault that they all think they can change me."

"Like moths to a flame they are," Cal said.

Hale and Cal's mother, Brea, chose that moment to glide over from the other half of their viewing box. Her flaxen hair was pulled into a sleek chignon and her coral dress was impeccably tailored. She looked no older than thirty, despite having two teenage sons. "Did you enjoy the race?"

"Hale did," Cal grumbled.

"The black?" Brea asked, glancing down at where the horse now stood with a garland of roses draped across its withers.

Hale nodded, puffing up with pride.

Brea laughed, a sweet, melodious sound. "You always were my good luck charm." She picked at a stray lock of his golden hair affectionately.

He shied away from her touch. "*Mother...*"

A wistful shadow passed across her smooth face. "I can't believe how big you boys are getting. Look at you. You're practically grown men."

"Some of us just think we're grown men," Cal said pointedly.

"Why don't you stand up and tell me that?" Hale said, standing to his not-insubstantial height of six and a half feet. "Though I'm not sure I'll be able to hear you from all the way up here."

Cal rocketed out of his chair, meeting Hale chest to chest. He couldn't stand that his baby brother had grown inches taller than him in the past few months. "It's easy to be tall when your head's filled with so much air. You're probably floating off the ground right now."

Brea let out a long-suffering sigh, throwing her hands up towards the heavens. "I don't know what I did to be punished with two boys. I could've had girls. Your mother did it right, Roan—one boy and three girls."

"I'm not sure my ma would agree," Roan said. "From all the screeching, it doesn't seem to be going well."

"But if I had girls, I could go shopping with them, go to tea parties…"

"You could do those things with Hale," Cal said with mock innocence. "He's pretty enough for tea and pastries."

"I thrive in all environments," Hale said. "It's not my fault your ugly face is only fit to be hidden in a library."

"Let's see how well you thrive after my fist spends some time in your face," Cal said playfully, smacking Hale upside the head. Hale met his brother's challenge with a headlock, and the two scuffled in a flurry of hooked elbows and knees.

"I turn my back for five minutes and this is what I return to find?" a deep voice thundered.

Hale and Cal broke apart in a flash, standing at attention before their father.

"Willum, they were only playing," Brea said, placing a soothing hand on her husband's forearm.

"That's all they ever do. When I was their age I was already serving as a page for Grand Minister Excentium." Hale's father was the Trade Minister for King Vespian of Aprica and seemed to object to anyone who did not take life as seriously as he did. *Especially* his youngest son.

"Clean yourselves up. We're late for lunch with Minister Turbino."

"Yes, sir," the brothers said in unison.

Hale's father spun on his booted heel and swept from the viewing box.

Hale sagged slightly as the tension in his spine that accompanied his father's presence uncoiled. "Do we have to go to lunch? All the ministers ever do is talk politics. I need to go collect my winnings," Hale said.

"If your father wants you there, you'll be there. End of story," Brea said.

"You should come too," Hale said to Roan, hoping his friend's presence would lessen the tedium of a lunch with the ministers.

"No, no, no. You couldn't rope me into that lunch for all the gold in Aprica. All the ministers will be complaining about the patricians. I'll be at lunch with my own kind. You know, where the patricians will be complaining about the ministers."

"The ministers wouldn't be complaining about the patricians if they would stop trying to overthrow the king," Hale said.

"Hale!" Brea said. "Don't say such things. You know the situation is complicated."

"Doesn't seem complicated to me. The king looks like death warmed over and the Grand Patrician has his eye on the throne. Simple."

Roan shrugged. "True enough. My dad's trying to stay out of things as best he can."

"Your father is an honorable man," Brea said. I'm sure Hale doesn't mean to suggest that he or any of the other patricians would do anything untoward."

"Oh no, nothing untoward." Hale laid a mocking hand over his chest. He snorted. "Evander's practically measuring the throne for his ass."

Even Cal sputtered a laugh at that one, but Hale's mother was not amused. "Enough! I will not hear one more word of this now and certainly not at lunch." She lowered her voice, so only Hale could hear her. "Do I need to remind you the consequences of embarrassing your father?"

Hale turned red, memories of leather belts flashing to the surface. "Fine. I'll be your boring perfect son. But just lunch. Then all bets are off."

"Lunch," Brea said with a world-weary sigh. "And when you come to visit my early grave remember this moment."

"Our mother could've had a career in the theater," Hale said to Cal, slinging his arm around his mother's narrow shoulders. "Her talents are wasted making wine."

"Don't drag me into this," Cal said, holding his hands up and backing away.

"Let's go." Brea patted Hale's chest. "We don't want to keep your father waiting."

Hale trailed after his mother and brother, descending the stairs from the shade of their viewing box. The purple blossoms of jacaranda trees filtered the sunshine, but the afternoon's heat was still powerful.

Roan peeled off from their group with a bump of his fist against Hale's. The racetrack was a proud old building of soaring spires and fluttering pennants. They had gone to the races as long as Hale could remember, to cheer for his uncle's racing stallions. Hale and Cal had both inherited their mother's love of animals—he remembered standing on the fences of the racing pens, watching as the horses were groomed. Hale's father, who to his knowledge didn't enjoy anything at all, tolerated the trips to the track, as it gave him an opportunity to network with other politicians.

As Hale had grown older, his attention had turned from the horses to other more interesting wildlife. Hale waggled his fingers at a clutch of passing girls who giggled and fluttered their handkerchiefs back in his direction. Hale grinned at his brother, who rolled his eyes. Hale smiled to himself. It wasn't his fault that the gods had smiled upon him in the looks department. If the young women of the city appreciated tall, well-built fellows with turquoise eyes and blond hair, who was he to dissuade them?

Hale was jarred from his daydream as his mother abruptly stopped before him. The brothers pulled up on either side of her, towering above her petite form.

"Sa Farina, it is a good day indeed when I have the opportunity to encounter such beauty." A thin older man dressed in the white smock of a chef stood before them, bowing low to kiss his mother's reluctantly proffered hand.

"Sim Daemastra, you are too kind," Brea said, using the male honorific.

"I swear you look lovelier and younger every time I see you. To think these two strapping young lads are your sons. You must tell me your secrets. You hardly look a day older than they."

"You flatter," Brea said with an uncomfortable laugh. "What brings you to the race track today, sir?"

Hale studied the man with a sick fascination as he droned on about his latest recipe. There was nothing for it—Eldo Daemastra creeped him the hell out. The man's smooth skin stretched too tight across his face, giving him a vaguely skeletal appearance. His teeth were too white and his hair was too thick for a man of his age. He was too nice, too friendly, too interested, especially in Hale's mother. While Hale had only met the Grand Patrician's personal cuisinier a few times, each encounter had left him with a distinctly uncomfortable impression.

Hale's mother seemed to feel the same. He could hear it in her uneasy laugh. Now the man was talking about getting his hands on some of Hale's mother's smallbatch wine, a vintage that was prized throughout the city—perhaps even all of Aprica.

Hale opened his mouth to come to her rescue, but it seemed that Cal had the same idea. "Mother, we don't want to be late for lunch. We should probably get going."

Yeah, you eerie old corpse, Hale thought.

"Of course. Shame on me for keeping you. I must attend to the patricians' lunch as well," Daemastra said, as if sharing a private joke. "You know how men get when their gazpacho is late."

"True. Important topics and empty stomachs are a dangerous combination."

Sim Daemastra raised one eyebrow, which seemed to float halfway up to his artificial hairline. "Important topics? Surely, the ministers are talking horse flesh and next week's regatta. That's all the patricians are discussing—I assure you."

"The same, the same. It was just a turn of phrase," Brea said.

"Mother..." Cal said, pulling his pocket watch from his unbuttoned waistcoat.

"Don't let me keep you. Brea, always a pleasure. Say *hello* to your husband for me."

Brea gave a stiff nod, and the cuisinier was gone. She wiped her hand on the fine brocade of her skirt. "That man is like a shadow passing across the sun."

"Was that a threat? 'Say *hello* to your husband for me,'" Hale said in a mocking tone, waggling his fingers at his mother.

"Don't be silly," Brea murmured. "Lunch awaits."

Hale met Cal's eye. Something was definitely up.

CHAPTER 2

Lunch was as tedious as Hale had predicted. Even worse, he had been forced to endure the entire afternoon cold sober—his father had cast him a thunderous look every time Hale so much as looked at the pitcher of wine. At least the food was good. The cuisinier had served a chilled watermelon, mint, and crumbled cheese salad followed by a pheasant glazed with orange and fennel reduction. The view wasn't so bad, either, with Minister Salta's daughter seated directly across from him. Her lace bodice had a swooping neckline, giving him a clear view of her sweet bosom every time she leaned forward to take a bite. He'd wondered idly if she was tempting him on purpose until her delicate toes creeping up the inside of his thigh made that fact perfectly clear.

Unfortunately, Hale's mother had spotted the girl's wandering toes when they made it too high, spoiling all his fun. When the lunch had come to a blessed end, Brea marched Hale down the stairs with a grip of surprising strength. He just managed to turn and throw the girl a roguish grin over his shoulder. Perhaps he would see her again. Courting women was rather like tending a garden. A little fertilizer here, some water there, and it was remarkable to see what would pop up.

The excitement of the afternoon's race was long gone, and now Hale found himself bored out of his mind at his family's villa, pacing before the wide double doors that overlooked the ornamental gardens. Brea sat at the table, delicate spectacles perched on her nose, going over a giant ledger filled with the accounts for her winery. His father had not returned with them, heading back to the palace for some late scheduled meeting of the ministers. Cal slouched in a chair by the empty fireplace, one long leg splayed over the arm, a book in his hands. Reading. He was always reading.

"Cal, you up for a game of pips?" The dicing game was Hale's favorite, but it required two to play. A betting game was no good without someone to take the money from.

"You always win," Cal said without looking up from his book.

"Is that a *yes?*" Hale asked, grabbing the book from his brother's hands. *The Rise of the Alesian Empire.* Boring.

"That's a *no.*" Cal snatched the book back. "Consider it a standing *no* for all eternity."

"And I thought being boring came naturally to you. It turns out you've been studying."

"Hale…" Brea said, not looking up from her ledger. "Leave your brother alone. If you can't find something to fill your time, I'm happy to find you some chores."

Cal snickered.

"Chores?" Hale was aghast. "That's what we have servants for."

Brea looked up, removing her spectacles. "It would be good for you to do some real work every now and then. Heavens only knows how you've grown so big when all you do is loaf around and eat."

"Mother! Don't forget my most important pastime—"

"Being an ass?" Cal said.

"Dazzling the city social scene." Hale made a face at his brother.

"Socializing is important, but it's not the type of labor I mean," Brea said. "Why don't you come to the winery with me tomorrow? We're pressing some of the grapes. You used to beg to come to the winery with me."

"I'm not eight years old anymore, Mother," Hale said. "I need a bit more than dusty floors and spider-filled vats of grapes to wow me these days."

Brea's face darkened. "Making wine is noble. It's science and it's art—it's romance and passion. I haven't sold out every vintage the last eight years for the spiders, I'll tell you that much."

The far doors burst open as Hale opened his mouth to make a halfhearted apology. It was Roan. He staggered into the room, his face ashen, his hair disheveled. "I ran all the way here." He gasped, resting his hands on his knees. "There's been a coup. The king is dead."

Brea's hand flew to her mouth in shock. Hale met his brother's eyes and saw his own worry mirrored there. What did this mean? For the country? For the ministers?

"The patricians?" Brea asked, though they all already knew the answer. Who else could it be? The patricians had been vying for power against King Vespian and his cabinet ministers for years now.

"Yes, Grand Patrician Evander led the charge himself. He has the military behind him as well. General Lysander has thrown his support behind him and the patricians. They're killing people."

"Killing people? Killing what people?" Hale asked.

Roan straightened and met Hale's eyes. The look of sympathy etched across his friend's face said more than words ever could. A rush of cold flooded Hale's body, numbing him to the core.

"Willum... He was at the palace..." Brea said faintly.

Cal was by his mother's side in three quick strides. "Roan. Tell us."

"I'm so sorry... There was fighting... The ministers tried to stop the general and his men. Sim Firena...he was killed. They all were."

"And now Evander sits on the throne..." Brea's voice was so light, it was as if it had been caught on a breeze. "First thing he will do is consolidate his power... eliminate..."

Roan nodded miserably. "I know this must be a shock, but you need to go. You need to get out of the city. It's not safe for you. Evander had sent soldiers into the city to round up everyone who was considered loyal to the late king. As the family of one of the most prominent ministers and his harshest critics, you'll be first on the list. That's why I came as fast as I could. I hoped I would get here before they did."

The ice in Hale's veins was slowly thawing, turning to fire. "And your father, what, just sat back while all this happened? While ministers were murdered? I'll bet he was in on it! Laughing behind our backs as he signed our death warrants!"

Roan shook his head wildly. "He didn't know—he didn't want this. He's been trying to get the Grand Patrician to see reason for years. This is on him."

"Hale—" Brea tried to place a soothing hand on his arm, but he shook it off.

"It's easy for him to say he had no part in it, but he'll be sitting pretty when this is all over, won't he? Your whole family will. Maybe you'd like our house." Hale gestured wide. "You can have my room." He knew the words were cruel even as they slipped between his lips. Roan had come to warn them after all. But it wasn't fair that his friend was standing here apologizing, while in one turn of fate Hale and his family had become fugitives.

His mother rounded on him, a look of fury on her face. "Hale Bartholomew Firena. That is enough. Roan came here at great personal risk. Let's not squander the chance he's given us." Her words doused the anger singing in his veins. Hale Bartholomew. It wasn't even his middle name. It was a trick she used from his childhood, when a silly name was all it had taken to turn a tantrum into a fit of giggles.

Brea continued. "Both of you—pack one bag with everything you might need. Be practical. There's no room for sentiment."

Hale and Cal stood for a moment before their mother flapped her hands at them. "Go!"

Hale took the stairs two by two. In his room, he found himself standing like a stone, unable to process what had happened. He should have been stuffing things into a sack, but all he could do was think about the fact that his father was dead. Emotions ripped through him. Yes, there was sorrow. But there was also…relief. Palpable relief that he would never see his father's disapproving face again. Guilt and hot shame followed. For what son feels relief upon hearing that his father is dead? A bang from Cal's room startled him out of his thoughts. Cal was already done packing. He needed to hurry.

First, clothing. He looked down at the tan linen trousers and white checked shirt that he still wore after the afternoon's race. Not practical for traveling. He stripped down to his small clothes and grabbed a pair of sturdy dark trousers, along with a shirt and waistcoat that he normally wore for pheasant hunting. He pulled on a pair of rich leather boots and grabbed his traveling cloak off its hook near the door.

Next, he grabbed a satchel from the wardrobe and looked around, wondering what to fill it with. It wasn't like he had the types of things one took on a journey, flint or fishing wire, or whatever travelers carried. He was a minister's son. In the end he settled on an extra pair of small clothes, another shirt, his tobacco pouch and rolling papers. His favorite pair of dice. His straight razor and a block of shaving cream. He pulled the ceremonial dagger his grandfather had given him off its stand on the shelf, fingering the flame of clan Farina on the pommel. Was the blade even sharp? He threw it in. If worse came to worst, he could fake his way out of a tight spot. He pulled a narrow-brimmed hat onto his head and surveyed the room. His satchel felt light. Far too light for a lifetime.

Brea and Cal were waiting for him at the bottom of the stairs. Both had changed into practical traveling clothes—dark colors and thick fabrics. They had sturdy boots and cloaks clasped around their necks. Roan had used the time to raid their kitchen. In one hand he held a bulging sack filled with food, in the other—three water skins.

Hale met Roan's eyes as he tossed over one of the water skins. "I'm sorry," Hale said. "Thank you. For coming."

"You would've done the same for me," Roan said, chewing his lip. "Be safe."

Brea was shouldering the sack of food when boots sounded on the stairs. She paled. "They're already here."

"Out the back. The servants' hallway," Cal said.

"Go," Roan said. "I'll try to distract them, send them the wrong way."

"We are in your debt," Brea said, squeezing his arm.

And then there was no time for goodbyes because the footsteps were growing louder. Hale led the way, rushing for the servants' door set into the far wall of the salon. As he grasped the knob, the door on the far side of the room flew open as well. There was no time to look back. Hale wrenched open the door before him. Silhouetted in the opening stood a soldier in blue, his naked blade glinting in the candlelight.

CHAPTER 3

Hale's thoughts spun like a top, mostly curse words making their way to the surface. *Bad, bad, this is bad.* He found himself backing away as the soldier advanced into the room. The man was big. As tall as Hale, but even broader of shoulder. His face was weathered, with a slice of a scar on his chin. His green eyes shone with uncomfortable intensity. But it was the sword that drew Hale's eye—sharp and wicked—gleaming like the last light of the sun before it slipped under the horizon. That sword wanted to kill him.

Hale hazarded a glance over his shoulder—but another soldier had appeared in the main doorway across the room. They were trapped. He looked back at the brute before him. Hale would be damned if he went down without a fight. The thought overtook him, and he moved on instinct. Hale didn't know a sword from a horse's ass, but he knew how to tackle. Hale launched himself at the soldier, aiming to catch the man in the gut with his not insubstantial shoulders. It didn't go as planned. Instead, inexplicably, he found himself grasped around the neck, flipped into the air, and smashed to the ground with shuttering crash. Glittering stars swam in Hale's vision as the air wooshed from his lungs.

"Normally, they give me the chance to say 'don't do anything stupid' before they try something stupid," the soldier said.

Hale wheezed, glaring at the man. How had the soldier moved so quickly?

"If I let you up, will you promise not to take another run at me? We're not here to hurt you."

"Says the man strangling me," Hale managed, his voice hoarse beneath the man's firm grip.

"Hale." His mother's voice cracked like a whip. "Do what the man says. Now is not the time to show off."

Hale reddened. He hadn't been trying to show off. He was trying to save their lives. Apparently, his mother was content to sit politely while she was executed. But Hale knew he wasn't much help from down here. He gave a curt nod.

The soldier stood and offered Hale a gloved hand. Hale ignored it, scrambling to his feet, rubbing at the back of his head where it had smashed against the travertine tile. He didn't feel any blood. He joined Cal and his mother in a taut semi-circle between the two soldiers. Roan stood flattened against the far wall, his eyes wild.

"Apologies for the dramatic entrance, Sa Firena," the man said, using the female honorific. "We wanted to make sure we got to you before someone else did. I take it from your traveling attire that you've heard about the unfortunate business at the palace."

"You mean the business where Evander slaughtered the rightful king and all his ministers, including my husband?" Brea said, her back straight, her head high.

All right, perhaps his mother wouldn't go politely, Hale amended.

The captain winced. "That business. I'm sorry to say Evander has gotten the taste for blood, and he's not yet spilled enough to slake his thirst. He's ordered all the ministers' families, including the three of you, to be rounded up and brought in."

Brea pursed her lips. "He means to make an example of us, no doubt."

"Your sons perhaps. But there's another reason I was sent here first, before the other families. It seems the Evander's cuisinier asked after you. You, my lady, are to be brought to him."

Brea blanched at the mention of Daemastra, and Hale didn't blame her. What did that walking skeleton want with his mother?

Cal stole the words out of Hale's mouth. "What does that creepy old bastard want with my mother?"

"I do not know, but I fear I would not be a man of honor if I allowed you to find out."

"Who sent you?" Brea asked.

"You have many friends among the military. Many who'd want you saved just so they wouldn't have to be without this year's burgundy blend. But it was General North. He sent me."

General North was an old friend of their family; he and Brea had grown up together. A man who brought them presents at Yuletide, and whom they had vacationed with in the summers. Often Hale's father had been too busy working to come along, and so it had been North who had taken the young boys fishing, had taught them to tie a line and gut a fish.

"Bless him," Brea said, the tension in her face melting somewhat.

"Unfortunately," the soldier continued, "he didn't have time to make arrangements for you. You'll have to find your own way out of the city. We can't be seen helping you."

"Can't—or won't," Hale muttered under his breath. For all the man's talk of honor, in the end he only cared about saving his own skin.

"Hale…" His mother shot a warning glance his way. "These men have done enough. They've risked themselves to give us a chance. We won't forget that. And we won't squander it either. What's the safest way out of the city?"

"The harbor," the man said. "All the roads will be guarded by Evander's soldiers. If you can make it through the city to the docks and onto a vessel headed out of Aprica, you might have a chance."

"A few captains export wine for me. I should be able to find us passage."

The soldier's next words were lost to the sound of pounding hooves on the cobblestones outside. Adrenaline flooded through him.

"Go," the soldier said. "We'll stall them as long as we can."

"Thank you both—you have risked much. Roan, come with us. At least until we're off of the villa estate. You shouldn't be found here. There would be too many questions."

Roan nodded.

A thunderous banging rang out from the front door below. Hale could just make out the muffled words. "Open up. In the name of the King!"

"Go!"

And then they were flying down the dark servants' hallway, out into the night. The boys pulled up short, flattening themselves against the stucco wall of the villa.

"Where's Mother?" Cal asked.

"She was just behind me...I thought..." Roan said.

Hale swore, plunging back through the doorway up the stairs. He almost bowled his mother over as he turned the dark corner towards the main part of the house. Behind her came the servants, many of them in their nightclothes. Fear was etched across their faces, ghostly in the shadowed light.

"What the hell are you doing?" Hale demanded.

"I had to tell them what was happening," Brea said. "It's up to them if they want to stay or go, but I couldn't leave without warning them. I don't know how far Evander's purge of our family will go."

Hale felt a surge of guilt, and then annoyance at the guilt. He hadn't even thought of the servants. But...he had a lot on his mind. Trying to stay alive and all. "Fine, but they're on their own. The more of us there are, the more conspicuous we are."

Brea nodded in agreement.

The muffled din of crashing furniture sounded from the house behind them. Evander's soldiers were turning the house upside down looking for them.

"Hurry," Brea said.

They dashed across the darkened courtyard towards the stables, trying to stay out of the yawning patches of light that stretched from the upper windows. Inside the stable, Hale grabbed three bridles off the hooks lining the stable wall. "There's no time to saddle the horses. Mother, can you ride bareback?"

Brea drew herself up to her full height, which barely came to Hale's chest. "Can I ride bareback? Do you take me for some pampered princess? I grew up on a horse ranch."

"It's just a question, Mother," Cal said, holding his hand out for a bridle.

Roan stood awkwardly in the corner as they hurriedly buckled the bridles.

"You can take a horse," Brea said. "We won't have need of them anymore."

"It's fine," Roan said. "It's less than a mile to my house. I'll be less conspicuous on foot."

A loud bang from the house made them all jump. "Now get out of here. Before the soldiers think to look in the stables. "

Hale clasped Roan's hand as he led his horse from the stall.

"Be safe," Roan said.

"Tell the ladies I did something heroic on my way out," Hale replied.

"They won't ever believe me," Roan said with a grin.

Hale grinned back before following his mother and brother out of the stable into the black night.

They led their horses to a side door in the villa's garden wall, cringing at every strike of hoof on stone. Once through the door, Hale offered his clasped hands as a step for his mother, and she launched herself nimbly onto the back of her chestnut mare.

Hale's heart hammered in his chest as they walked through the dark city, not wanting to draw the attention that a panicked gallop might bring. Every person they passed brought a new wave of tension and fear, as if this might be the time that they would be recognized, that someone would call after them to stop. But no one did. Brea led the way through the twisting streets, sticking to back alleys and dark residential roads. Hale wasn't sure how she knew her way around the city; when he and Cal came into town, they almost always took the family carriage.

The verdant rolling hills of the Villa District descended into the main part of Se Caelus, the capital and government seat of Aprica. They passed the downtown shopping district—the city center where merchant guilds met and traded. The city was eerily quiet, but for the sound of boots pounding in the distance. It seemed that word of the coup had spread, and the city's inhabitants weren't taking any chances.

Hale worried at the reins, wiping his sweaty palms on his legs. The silence of the night—of their ride—was oppressive, but every time he opened his mouth to speak, Cal or his mother would shoot him a warning glance. The tension coiled around his spine began to loosen as he caught his first whiff of the briny sea air. The cries of gulls joined the rhythm of their horses' hooves. They were close.

Finally, they arrived at the docks that stretched along Se Caelus's harbor like jutting fingers. Blessedly, the harbor appeared to be empty of Evander's troops. Brea drew her horse to a stop in front of a proud schooner flying the sky blue Aprican flag. "Let me do the talking." She slipped off her mount with a graceful swing and handed the reins to Hale.

A tall, broad-shouldered man with a black goatee and a red high-collared coat strode down the docks to meet them. "Sa Farina, to what do I owe the pleasure?" He took her hand and bowed low over it, polite despite the second question implied by his tone: *And what is the wife of one of the city's most prominent ministers doing at the harbor at midnight?*

"We're looking to arrange passage out of the city," Brea said. "Can you assist us?"

"I'm afraid our new *king*"—the man said the word with a twist of distaste—"has closed the harbor. No boats in or out."

Cal and Hale exchanged a glance. Not good.

"For how long?"

The man must've seen the dismay on Brea's face. "I'm sorry, my lady. I don't know. There may be... never mind. It would be too risky for a lady such as yourself."

"Tell me."

"I've heard there's a man who will be leaving. His cargo is such that...he doesn't want to draw undue attention."

"A smuggler?" Brea asked.

The captain nodded, a look of apology on his face, as if Hale's mother was so delicate that the very notion of smuggling would offend her.

"Where is he berthed?"

The captain pointed down the row of ships. "Single mast down the line. Red hull."

"I thank you," Brea said, turning to leave.

"My lady," the captain said, threading his fingers together nervously. "Such men are not to be trusted. I do not know if that vessel would be safe for a respectable lady such as yourself. If you could just wait... I could try to arrange alternate passage—"

"Your chivalry is admirable, but put your conscience at ease," Brea said. "There's no safe place for us now."

CHAPTER 4

The vessel flew no colors. Its lacquered hull shone scarlet in the moonlight—but what looked as ominous as blood from afar revealed itself to be flaking off in shabby patches as they drew closer. Though Hale would have much preferred the grand schooner they had left behind farther up the dock, the little ship looked sturdy enough. Men swarmed the deck and up the rigging, one shouldering past them as he carried cargo onto the vessel. By all appearances, the ship was leaving any minute.

"Is your captain aboard?" Brea asked a barefooted sailor who hurried by. Without pausing, he gestured towards the stern with a nod of his chin.

Brea slid to the ground. "Hold the horses, Hale." She handed him the reins before making her way up the gangplank.

"Hold the horses, Cal," Hale said, tossing the reins to his brother before jogging after his mother.

"Hey!" Cal called after him.

Brea let out a long-suffering sigh as Hale caught up with her. He offered his most charming smile in return.

"Let me do the talking," she said. "I don't need you offending him somehow."

"Offending him?" Hale said with mock innocence. "When have I ever offended anyone?"

Brea's retort was swallowed by a gruff voice.

"Who the hell are ye?"

The captain looked every inch a pirate. Well, Hale assumed this man was the captain, because no one else could get away with slouching against the rail with such a look of disdain. And he assumed this is what a pirate would look like, from his few times patronizing the theater. From the top of the man's tricorne hat, plumed with a peacock feather, to the tips of his worn leather boots, the man fit the part. He held a map in one hand (an honest-to-god pirate map?) and the nub of a rolled cigarette in the other.

"Hello," Brea said brightly, as if running into an old friend at the market. "We're hoping to buy passage."

"Passage to where?" the captain asked, taking a long drag on his cigarette before blowing the smoke into Brea's and Hale's faces.

Hale narrowed his eyes. Who did this man think he was to disrespect them so?

Brea laughed, as if untroubled by the cloud of tobacco smoke wafting about her glossy curls. "That depends. Where are you headed?"

"As far away from this coup business as I can get. New monarchs always want to flex their power. Inspections, taxes. I think we'll head south for a while."

"Tamros? We would be happy to secure passage to Tamros."

The captain flicked the end of his cigarette overboard and hooked his thumb in his sword belt. "No can do. Ye'll have to find yerself another ship."

Hale's gaze fell on the captain like a lead weight. This man could not say *no* to them. They needed out of the city. They would get on this boat, the easy way, or the hard way.

"Why not?" Brea asked. "We can pay. We won't be any trouble."

The captain met Hale's gaze, his dark eyes issuing a silent challenge.

Hale didn't back down and met the man's eyes with a stare of his own.

The captain chuckled. "Ye sure?"

"Hale," Brea hissed. "Be polite."

"Just returning the hospitality of our host," Hale said with a forced smile.

The captain grinned in return, a smile filled with half as much gold as tooth.

"Ow," Hale hissed as Brea stomped on his foot with her booted heel.

"Women are bad luck at sea. Won't have one on the Nightingale," the captain said. "And I reckon ye bring worse luck than most."

"I can't imagine what you mean," Brea said.

"I suspect I'm talking to someone in fine clothes, with three horses worth more than my boat, out here in the middle of the night, desperate to buy passage out of Aprica. Someone who may be of interest to our new monarch. Am I close?" The captain narrowed his eyes. "Like I said. Don't need more bad luck."

Brea soldiered on, ignoring the captain's admonishments. "Surely, the right amount of gold can banish even the worst luck. As I see it, you've got something in your hold you don't want the new king to see; otherwise, you wouldn't be risking running the blockade in the dead of night. Am I close?"

The captain grunted and looked away, chewing on the inside of his cheek.

"So what's one more piece of illicit cargo in your hold? Think of it as…hazard pay."

"It'd have to be *some* hazard pay…" The captain squinted.

Brea reached into a pouch at her waist and pulled out her diamond wedding ring. The diamond was the size of a quail's egg and had been the envy of every lady in the Aprican court.

The captain let out a low whistle, his black eyes glinting.

"Mother, no," Hale said. "Father would roll over in his grave."

"I don't think they'll do him the honor of a grave," she said softly. "It's just a thing. You boys are all that matter to me now." Brea straightened, squaring her shoulders. "It's yours if you get us safely to Tamros. Do we have an accord?"

"We do, me fine lady," the captain said, his golden smile widening as he flourished a bow that would have made a patrician proud. He straightened and reached for the ring with eager fingers.

"After you get us safely to Tamros," Brea said, whisking the ring back into her pouch. "And not a minute sooner."

The captain smirked, as if a bit impressed with the woman before him. Hale was a little impressed himself. He knew his mother was a businesswoman, selling some of the most sought-after vintages in all of Aprica, but he had never seen her in her element.

"The last of the cargo is loaded, Captain." A sailor approached, a colorful kerchief tied over his brow to keep his long, dark locks out of his face. Hale wasn't used to men with such long hair, but many of the sailors on deck seemed to prefer the fashion. He rather liked the look of it.

"We need to get my other son," Brea said.

"Ye have three minutes before we cast off," the captain said. "Be on the Nightingale or be left behind."

Brea and Hale jogged back down the gangplank as the sound of unfurling sails snapped behind them.

Cal was waiting with barely restrained anticipation where they had left him. "What happened?"

"He'll take us to Tamros. We leave now," Brea said. "Let's go."

"What about the horses?" Cal asked.

"Leave them," Brea said. "Someone will find them. They'll make their way to good homes."

"Leave them?" Cal said, looking up and down the docks. "They're bound to get cut up for dinner around this lot."

"There's no time, Cal," Hale said, giving his chestnut, Jasper, a last stroke on his nose. Hale wasn't crazy about horses the way his brother was, but Jasper had been a good horse. Regal. Proud. They had looked good together.

"Mother," Cal said, a waver in his voice. "I've raised Stone since he was a foal. I can't just abandon him."

"Oh, Cal, my sweet Cal." Brea sighed, reaching up to cup Cal's cheek in her hand. "I know he is your friend, but he is a beast. To waste even a minute is to trade your life for his. He would not ask this of you, would he?"

"No," Cal said slowly, resting his forehead against his horse's, looking into the two dark pools of his horse's eyes.

A thick rope thunked on the dock next to them, making Hale jump.

"Casting off!" a sailor shouted.

"Now, Cal," Brea said, grabbing Cal's hand and wrenching him away from the horses, which stamped in confusion on the dock.

They ran up the gangplank and leaped onto the deck as two sailors pulled the wooden boards up behind them.

Cal ran to the side as the wind filled the sails, pulling the ship away from the dock.

The flickering lights of Se Caelus grew smaller as the ship slid through the dark waters of the marina, leaving a rippling wake across the inky blackness of the water. Hale turned from the city to find a small sailor watching him from across the busy deck, a rope held motionless in his hands. The boy must've been younger than Hale…thirteen, maybe fourteen. His red hair glinted as bright as the lantern-light, and his eyes shone green even across the space between them. The intensity of the boy's scrutiny unnerved him somehow. As if the lad was taking his measure…and found him wanting.

Hale narrowed his eyes. Who did this urchin think he was, to challenge Hale Firena? He was the son of the trade minister of Aprica…part of a proud noble clan that had helped settle these lands. "What're you looking at, boy?" Hale barked across the deck, his face warming. "Don't you have work to do?"

"Ye." The captain whirled, pulling a curved dagger from his belt and leveling it at Hale. "Talk to me crew again and I'll throw ye overboard. I don't care if yer mother pays me all the gold in Aprica. On this vessel, ye're no one."

Hale's righteous indignation spluttered and died at the captain's words. The events of the evening came crashing down upon him. Adrenaline from their flight swirled from him like water down a drain, leaving Hale hollow and empty. On this boat or off, he was no one. Not anymore. His father was dead. The Firena clan was an enemy of the crown. They were fugitives.

"Now, boy, don't ye have work to do?" the captain barked at the small sailor, who scurried back to work.

"You three, come here," the captain said, gathering Hale and his family with a gesture. They formed a tight circle around him.

"I'm Captain Brimmer. The trip to Tamros will be a week, if the winds favor us. Ye'll stay below. There's a cabin—it's filled with cargo, but push it to the side and ye should be able to hang a few hammocks. Don't trouble me men, and you'll not be troubled by 'em. Especially you, me lady. I keep a tight ship, but men will be men. I wouldn't wander about without one of these lads around. Understood?"

"Understood," Brea said, her chin held high.

"We'll be passing through the harbor gates in five. We'll be going dark and quiet, and hope we aren't noticed. Get below. Not a peep from ye, ye hear?"

"There's no need to talk to us like children," Hale said. "We understand Aprican."

"I treat ye like children when ye act like them." The captain stepped forward until his chest nearly touched Hale's. Hale was taller, but the man had a presence about him, a casual menace that spoke of dark deeds and secrets buried. It took all of Hale's self-control to stand his ground.

"We understand," Brea said, laying a hand on Hale's arm. "We'll get below." Her grip tightened on his forearm until her nails dug into his flesh.

Hale stepped back, spinning and stalking across the ship, ducking down the stairs into the hold.

"Is it possible for you to go five seconds without getting into a dick-measuring contest with someone?" Cal exploded at Hale the moment they were below. "I swear to the gods, it's a miracle you haven't gotten us killed already. It's not like father can come bail you out of jail this time."

"I know." Hale met the fire in Cal's eyes with his own. "Because he's dead. Someone's got to look out for this family now."

"Boys," Brea said. "I will be taking care of this family now. And Hale, I know you mean well, but Cal is right. We need to lay low until we make it to Tamros. We can't afford to make any more enemies. Understood?"

"If Cal had his way, we'd be smiling and bowing while we all had our throats cut."

"I *said,* understood?" Brea's voice was quiet. It was a bad sign when her voice got quiet. "This is not up for discussion."

"Understood," Hale grumbled.

"Good," she said. "Now let's find our cabin."

Their cabin turned out to be a virtual closet that wasn't worthy of the name, even if it hadn't been piled high with boxes and barrels.

"Where are we supposed to sleep?" Hale asked.

"At least it has a window," Cal said, clambering over a box to look out the tiny porthole. "Hey. We're near the breakwater. But…it doesn't look like we're moving."

"Let me see," Hale said, shoving his brother aside. The porthole was grimy with salt, and he squinted to see through to the blackness beyond. Another vessel glided into view, its hull painted the sky blue and gold of the Aprican monarchy.

"There's another boat," Hale said.

"What?" Brea asked, her voice tense.

He peered out again, blinking through the salty haze. Iron fingers thrust out of the side of the other vessel. Cannons. Hale's mouth went dry as a spark of a flint flashed across the water.

"Get down!"

CHAPTER 5

A cannonball exploded through the wall of the ship in a shower of splinters and sparks. Hale pressed himself to the deck, squeezing his eyes closed as debris rained upon them. The smell of gunpowder singed his nostrils. Someone was firing on them! The thought filled him with a kind of giddy excitement. This would be an adventure to talk about.

When it seemed that the worst of the shrapnel had fallen, Hale risked raising his head. His mother and Cal were pressed to the ground next to him, covered in a layer of sawdust and wood. A hole the size of a wine barrel gaped in the ship's side. Their attacker was visible. And more sparks were being struck. Another cannon.

The second cannonball struck the bow of the Nightingale with a teeth-rattling impact. "We need to get out of here," Hale said, using a nearby crate to pull himself to his feet. "Now."

Cal protested. "The captain said to stay below."

"That was before someone was firing at us! Feel free to stay here and die, but I'm going. Mother, come on." Hale helped Brea to her feet. He had never seen her shaken before, but now, with pieces of wood and sawdust littering her tresses, she seemed unnerved.

"Let's go, Cal," Brea said. "We don't want to be down here if the ship starts to sink."

Brea's words proved prophetic. As they rounded out of the cabin into the dark hallway, Hale's boots sloshed through shallow water pouring from deeper in the hold. Hale helped Brea up the ladder onto deck first, following close behind to catch her if another cannonball hit. Chaos reigned on deck. The Nightingale had almost made it through the breakwater of the harbor out into the bay, but two schooners bearing the colors of the Royal Navy were now flanking them, firing at will. The little ship's mast had been hit and was leaning unnaturally, like a bone out of joint. Sailors dashed about with shouts and buckets of water, trying to put out a fire that was spreading across the stern.

"What happened?" Hale grabbed the captain's arm as he stalked by, barking orders at his men.

"I hoped to slip out undetected. We didn't. They started shooting."

"Can we make it through?" Brea asked. "Escape?"

"They could outrun us even if we weren't taking on water and fulla holes. Hope ye fancy lords and ladies can swim. Griff!" He shouted at the tiny boy. "Bring us around. Why're we giving 'em such a big target?"

Griff didn't have a chance to take more than a few steps when a cannonball crashed across the top of the deck like a stone skipping across a pond. It bowled through one unfortunate sailor, tossing his mangled body into the air before burying itself in the Nightingale's mast.

"She's going over!" Captain Brimmer shouted as the mast bellowed a deep groan. "Get down!"

Hale fell to the deck beside his mother, covering her with his body as best he could. He caught Cal's gaze beside him—his eyes wild and panicked. The mast creaked again, a long keening sound like the death knell of some otherworldly beast. And then it toppled into the sea with a reverberating splash, pulling ropes and rigging and cleats with it.

Hale coughed, dust and smoke stinging his eyes and filling his lungs. The fire from the stern was spreading, licking its way up the leaning decks towards the front of the boat. Another cannon exploded from the ship to their right, blinding Hale temporarily with a violent flash. The shot hit low against the waterline of the ship's bow, shuddering the deck once more.

"We need to get out of here," Hale said. "This boat is going down. Mother, what should we do? Head back to the docks? Hope we can find another way out?"

It seemed the madness of the night had finally caught up with Brea. Her face was pale, her eyes wide and vacant. She was going to be no help.

"Evander's men will be waiting for us back there." Cal groaned. "This escape plan was never going to work."

"They don't have us yet," Hale said, cracking his knuckles. He hated to admit it, but Cal was right. Heading back to the dock was suicide. He looked around for an idea, an inspiration, trying to see past tongues of flame snaking into the air, the smoke that stung his eyes. A rowboat. There was a rowboat being lowered into the water. The captain's tricorne hat was just visible through the flames. The man was abandoning ship. Wasn't a captain supposed to go down with his vessel?

"A boat!" Hale pointed. "Let's go!" Hale grabbed his mother's arm and yanked her forward, clamoring over the rigging and the shattered mast, shying away from flames that reached for them with greedy fingers. The fire roared like a furnace, so hot Hale was sure his skin would blister. But they stumbled forward, collapsing against the railing where the captain stood. The skiff was already in the water, filled with eight crewmen.

"Let us in the boat," Hale said.

"It's full," Captain Brimmer said. "Shove off. May ye find easy seas and easy women," he called down to his men, dropping the ropes from the side of the rail.

"Please. At least...my mother."

"Ye don't want your ma alone with eight lonely sailors," the captain said. "She'll have better luck prayin' to the Piscator for mercy. I suggest you get swimming. Or die here. Your choice. Come on, Griff. Can't stick around here no more." With that, Captain Brimmer removed his hat and jumped off the side of the boat into the black water below.

The small sailor who had stared at Hale appeared out of nowhere, an apparition in the smoke. "He's right," the boy said quietly. He had a quiet, lilting voice, almost musical in quality. "Stay too long and the ship'll suck you down when it goes." Then he dove into the water—a perfect arrow shot into the black. He surfaced some yards off, stroking strong and sure towards the breakwater.

The breakwater. A sudden thought lit Hale's mind like a shooting star. "Come on," he said. "We follow them. Swim for the breakwater, then make our way across it back to land, but climb down outside the city."

"Okay," Cal said, shoving his blond hair out of his eyes.

"Mother, are you strong enough to swim?" Hale shook her gently. "Mother, we need you to be strong for a while longer. Don't let that bastard Evander win."

That seemed to bring her back to herself. Her gaze focused, and she met Hale's eyes. "I can swim." She took her cloak off and quickly stuffed it in her pack before donning the pack again and tightening the straps. Hale raised an eyebrow at Cal, and they quickly followed their mother's example. The cloaks would be heavy when waterlogged.

The ship was listing now and Hale and Cal had to help their mother up on the railing. She looked back, her tan skin glinting in the firelight. "We stay together," she said before diving into the water almost as gracefully as the sailor boy.

Hale and Cal's entrances were considerably less elegant. Hale tucked himself into a ball and crashed against the water with a great splash while Cal half-flopped, half-dove. They surfaced and bobbed in the water, each accounting for the others. From here, the damage to the Nightingale was the stuff of nightmares—its once-glossy flanks burst open in ragged holes, its proud rigging limp and tangled.

Hale turned from the sight and followed Brea and Cal towards the breakwater. Another boom sounded, a cannon shot bursting from the nearest Aprican schooner. "They're still firing," Hale said, panting as he looked back at the Nightingale. But they weren't firing at the ship. The little rowboat bearing most of the Nightingale's crew was blasted into the air in a column of water and boards and bodies.

"All those men..." Cal said, floundering for a moment, his eyes reflecting the flames billowing from the wreckage of the skiff.

"Can't...do anything for them now..." Hale panted. "Shore..." Briny water lapped into his mouth and he sputtered, coughing.

Brea was the first to begin the swim towards shore once again, slipping silently past them with measured strokes. There was nothing for him and Cal to do but follow.

Hale knew he had reached the breakwater when he bashed his shin against a submerged rock. He let out a spluttered curse, treading water and trying not to make any more sudden movements. The breakwater was a ring of man-sized granite boulders piled on top of each other. It was intended to keep unwelcome ships and excess waves from the city's harbor. Tonight, it had saved their lives.

Hale turned and offered his brother a hand, hauling him onto the rocks. Brea had already climbed onto the nearest rock and was wringing water from her curls. Her face was pale in the moonlight.

"Are you cold, Mother?" Cal asked, not that there was anything they could do about it.

"I will be fine, my son," Brea said with a hand to Cal's cheek. "Let's get moving. It will warm us."

They picked their way carefully along the boulders of the breakwater, traversing the curving arc that led to shore. For a few minutes, Hale's mind grew numb to anything but the squelch of water in his boots and the gentle lapping of the waves. From time to time, Cal would look back at the blaze that still roared merrily over the wreckage of the Nightingale. Hale didn't want to look back anymore. Forward. Keep moving forward.

The breakwater met the shore along the city's wall. A guard tower was posted there, standing like a tall sentinel in the darkness. Men's voices emanated from within the open air of the tower's balcony, words drifting down like ash on the breeze.

Hale held up a finger to his lips and pointed down towards the far side of the breakwater, where the rocks met the beach outside the city's stern walls. He went first, his eyes locked on the tower above, praying no stray soldier poked his head out to survey the world below.

"Ow!" A muffled cry sounded as Hale stepped on something soft. Something that was most definitely not a rock.

"Captain?"

"Aye, who the hell else would it be? Not enough that ye blew up me ship, ye have to break me hand too?"

"We didn't blow up your ship," Hale hissed, peering in the dark. The captain wasn't alone. The small sailor boy was with him. They were crouched in the dark, the captain's pant leg rolled up while the boy wrapped a bandana around a wound. "We just happened to be there when the boat blew up. Are you injured?"

"A scratch." The captain waved away Hale's concern. "'Tis nothing."

The boy shook his head in exasperation.

"Captain." Brea had caught up. "I'm glad you're alive."

"That makes two of us."

"How do you plan on getting out of the city?"

"I've contacts…"

"Take us with you," Brea said. "There's still a diamond ring in it for you if you help us get out of Se Caelus. Big enough to buy a new ship. Hire a new crew."

The captain seemed to ponder this, exchanging a conversation in a look with the boy. A dark expression crossed across the boy's face, but the gleam in the captain's eye at the mention of the egg-sized diamond seemed to dissuade him.

"Fine," Captain Brimmer said. "I know a trader who runs caravans to Tamros. He's leaving tomorrow. I get you on his caravan, and the diamond is mine."

"You get us on the caravan and safely to Tamros, and the diamond is yours."

"Only a fool makes the same deal twice," the captain said. "At least when it almost got him killed the first time."

The sailor boy seemed to agree, glaring at Hale with those green eyes.

"A rich fool," Brea said softly.

CHAPTER 6

The darkness clawed at Hale as they made their way through the labyrinth of rundown buildings and houses nestled against the Se Caelus walls. He wrinkled his nose as they slipped between leaning shacks and stepped over piles of gods-only-knew-what. How did people live like this? Disgusting.

His clothes were stiff and scratchy from the drying salt; his boots were still squelching with seawater, rubbing his heels raw. Hale looked over his shoulder at the harbor, the wreck of the ship still smoking, casting a tangerine glow upon the dark water.

"I told you we shouldn't have left the horses." Cal grumbled next to him. His brother's blond hair was plastered to his forehead, hanging in his eyes, but he didn't seem to care enough to brush it aside. Perhaps Cal was numb with the shock of all of that had happened that night.

"We couldn't have known the boat would get blown up," Hale said.

A hissing noise came from the captain, and when Hale looked up, the man made a sharp gesture across his mouth, signaling them to be silent.

Hale glowered at the man, wishing they didn't need him. There was no way they could trust this smuggler—everyone knew pirates had no honor. Hale was sure that it was only his mother's diamond ring that was keeping the man from turning them over to the Aprican guard, and perhaps even that wouldn't be enough. If Evander set a sizable reward for their capture, what would stop him from turning on them? Hale would have to keep an eye on the man. If…when…the captain tried to double-cross them, he'd be ready.

As the night wore on and the rubbing in Hale's boots gave way to full-on blisters, they joined a small but steady stream of people leaving the city. It seemed that they and the captain weren't the only ones made nervous by the change in leadership. Hale watched those around them from the dark recess of his hood. Where would these people go? Stay with friends? Families? Try to make the journey to Tamros? The road was notoriously dangerous, as the Tamrosi government was unstable and lacked the coin or backbone to deal with the warring bands of brigands who preyed on travelers in the woods. These people were embarking on a difficult and dangerous road.

"Hale," his mother said, and Hale's head snapped around, looking for her. There. They had taken a turn off the main road, up a side street. He turned and hurried to join his mother and Cal.

"Captain Brimmer says the caravan gathers at a large inn up this road. It's not much farther," she said.

"An inn?" Hale asked hopefully. He didn't think he had ever felt this weary in his life.

"I doubt we'll have much time to rest," Brea said apologetically. "The captain thinks the caravan is leaving at dawn."

"Maybe we can sleep in the wagons," Cal said hopefully.

"Ye lazy asses can sleep when yer dead." Captain Brimmer had stopped and turned, fists on his belted hips. "Which'll be soon if ye don't pick up the pace. We miss this caravan, good luck getting to Tamros without getting yer milky white throats slit."

Hale bristled, stepping forward. "Don't use such language in front of my mother."

Brea put a hand on Hale's chest. "Hale, it's fine. Not everything's worth a fight."

"Listen to yer mother, young pup," Brimmer said. "Or yer not gonna last very long out there in the real world."

Brea sent a long-suffering look the captain's way. "Can we just get there?"

"Fine by me." The man turned on his heel and continued marching up the hill, a slight hitch in his step from the gash on his leg. The redhaired boy, Griff, stared at Hale a beat longer before turning to follow. Why was that boy always staring?

Brea wrapped her hand around Hale's arm, tugging him forward. "Soon this will seem like a distant nightmare."

Hale swallowed his retort. He hoped his mother was right. Because he had a sinking feeling that their nightmare was just beginning.

Hale longed to put his hands on his knees and gasp for breath when the inn came into view, perched like an eagle at the top of the hill. His pride didn't allow it. Perhaps in the future he would do a bit more endurance work, in addition to lifting weights with the guards. The inn was a wide U-shape of red stucco buildings curling around the central grassy courtyard. A row of wagons paralleled the stables, hitched to pairs of brown horses standing patiently, munching from feed bags strapped to their noses.

The captain swaggered forward through two double doors into the lobby of the inn, the rest following quickly behind. The room housed a small desk, chair, and cozy couch across from a fireplace, which was blazing merrily. The aroma of meat wafted in from the common room, which was visible through the hallway. Hale's mouth watered. He was starving.

"Here to see Sim Chiron," Captain Brimmer said to a pretty brunette behind the desk.

The woman took them all in with bright unflinching eyes. "He expecting you?"

Hale resisted the urge to straighten his wrinkled, stained shirt.

"No, but we're not here to cause trouble. Want to join his caravan, if he'll have us."

"He's finishing breakfast," the woman said, pointing down the hallway and turning back to her ledger.

The captain turned to them, adjusting his hat over his brow. "Let me do the talking, right?"

Hale wasn't sure what he expected a trader to look like, but Sim Chiron was not it. Even more surprising was his reaction when he caught sight of Captain Brimmer.

The man was on his feet in a blink, the coffee in his mug jostling onto the table. "Captain Brimmer, you treasonous snake. The last time I saw you, you traded me a dozen barrels of sugar full of weevils!"

The captain had his hands up. "That was never me intent. And I've brought ye something far more valuable to make up for any grief I may have caused ye."

The man turned his appraising eye on Hale and his family standing awkwardly behind the captain.

"Can't hurt to hear me out before ye kill me, right?" The captain grinned, the gold in his teeth glinting in the morning sunlight.

The man barked a laugh and came around the table to clap the captain on the back in a hug. "You do keep things interesting. All right. Join me for a cup of coffee. That lady too. The rest of your men can grab some breakfast from the kitchen."

Hale opened his mouth to protest, but a look from his mother silenced him. He settled for glowering at the man.

"Come on," Griff said, turning on his heel. Hale was hungry. It couldn't hurt to get a meal in him.

After retrieving a cup of pungent coffee and a plate of questionable eggs and gnarled bacon, Hale, Cal, and Griff sat down at the table nearest to the others. The captain appeared to be talking up Hale's mother to the caravan trader. The man was as tall as Hale, but much thicker in the middle, with the blond hair of an Aprican pulled back in a ponytail. Perhaps he might have been a soldier, back in his youth. He had a hard look to him, and his left ear had a notch taken out of the lobe.

"Do you think we can trust him?" Hale asked Cal in low tones, his eyes narrowed.

"Don't think we can trust anyone," Cal said glumly, shoveling a bite of eggs into his mouth. "No offense, Griff."

"None taken," Griff replied. The lad had almost finished his whole plate already. Where did he put it? "What's your plan once you get to Tamros?"

"None of your concern," Hale replied, pulling apart his bacon with a savage bite. Who knew bacon could even be this tough? Had the pig done hard labor in a work camp?

"So…no plan then," Griff replied.

"Have you been to Terrasia?" Cal asked, referring to the capital city of Tamros.

Griff nodded once, his smooth face going stony. "Once. I don't intend to go back."

"That bad?" Cal asked with dismay.

"We don't have to settle there," Hale said, taking a sip of coffee and practically gagging. How was it possible to even make food this bad? "We could go on to Alesia."

"I've heard Maradis is nice—" Cal said, but he was interrupted by Brea, who appeared at their side.

"They've agreed to let us come." She paused. "But there's a complication. A few complications."

"What?" Cal asked.

"You two will be working for Sim Chiron until we get to Terrasia."

"Working?" Hale said, his tone laced with horror. "Like common folk? Why?"

Griff snickered but did his best to cover it with a cough. Hale glowered at him.

"He said that his men don't wait on anyone. If we want to go, we will do our part. I, for one, think it will be good for you."

"I'm sure you do," Hale muttered.

"You said there were a few complications?" Cal asked.

"The new king has set up a roadblock on the Tamrosi border. Anyone who crosses, anything that crosses, will be searched."

Hale swore. "Bloody hell. We're doomed then, aren't we? If this slop is the last meal I have, I'm going to have some serious words with the

Sower when I die."

"I think we know it'll be the Huntress coming for you," Cal said. "You're far too pretty for her to spare an eternity of torment and suffering."

"Boys, please." Brea sighed, rubbing her temples with a hand. "Now, Sim Chiron has indicated that he has at times had to transport certain...items of a sensitive nature in his wagons. He has space where we can hide while we pass the border check."

Hale raised his eyebrows appraisingly. "What is the sensitive nature of the items?" He mused.

"Drugs," Griff said quietly. "Don't cross him."

Hale's eyebrows went up even higher. "This trip just got interesting."

"I don't think you'll get to sample the merchandise," Cal said.

"Hale—" Brea said with a warning tone.

"Mother, relax," Hale said, standing and laying his hands on his mother's sagging shoulders. "I'll behave myself. I'll be just as boring as Cal for the whole rest of the trip, I promise. And when we cross the border, I'll cuddle some drugs in a tiny false bottom on a moving wagon like a perfect gentleman. What could go wrong?"

Brea dropped her forehead against Hale's chest. "What could go wrong indeed."

CHAPTER 7

The caravan consisted of six covered wagons pulled by teams of horses, eight men, three women (including one very pretty girl), and a spotted brown dog. After Sim Chiron had finished his coffee, the caravan set off at an amble up the road from the inn. Hale's family walked alongside the wagons, which seemed incredibly inefficient to Hale. What were wagons for if not to ride on?

"I swear I've done more walking in the last twenty-four hours than in my entire life." Hale grumbled under his breath, dancing out of the way of a spray of gravel kicked up by the nearest wagon.

"That's cuz you're a spoiled ass," Cal said, but Hale could tell his heart wasn't in it. His gaze was fixed on the ground before him, his steps slow and shuffling. Hale glanced at his mother, who walked mutely alongside Cal. Her hair was wild and one cheek was streaked with dirt. For a woman normally so meticulous about her beauty routine, it was an alarming admission of defeat.

Hale sank into brooding silence beside them, watching the scrubby scenery. The adrenaline of their flight from Se Caelus had dimmed, and the stark reality of their situation was beginning to set in. No home. No allies. No income. No more lavish parties, no more carousing with friends, no more attracting ladies like moths to a flame. No more Hale Firena. Not really. He was still standing, but Hale Firena, what that name meant—the privilege and prestige—that man was gone, surely as if he had been shot in the skiff, rowing for shore. Who was he, if he wasn't Hale Firena? He didn't know, and even if he had known, he wasn't sure he'd like the answer.

And then there was his father. The reality his mind danced around, recoiling every time it so much as touched those roiling emotions. His father was dead. Surely he could muster some sorrow, some sadness that the man who had given him life, had given him his name, had left this world.

"You two!" Chiron barked, pointing at them from the wagon ahead. The man had buckled on a sword belt and wrapped his neck with a gray and white checked scarf. He looked even more intimidating out here than he had sitting in the inn's common room. Cal and Hale exchanged a look and jogged over to meet the man.

"Your mother said you're willing to work to earn your way. Yes?"

"We weren't really presented with a choice in the matter," Hale groused under his breath, crossing his arms.

"Yes, sir," Cal said, glaring at Hale. "What can we do?"

"Let me introduce you," Chiron said. They followed the man to the front wagon, where two men rode behind a team of bay horses. *See, these men were allowed to ride!* "This is Stiv and Hamilton," he said, pointing to a burly man with close-cropped fair hair and a lanky fellow with straggly locks and a dark goatee. "They keep this caravan running. They're your bosses. They say jump, you ask how high. Understood?"

Hale suppressed a snort. He jumped for no man. But he gave a curt nod to keep Chiron from giving him a hard time.

"Who are the others?" Hale asked, pointing back at the last wagon, where the pretty blonde girl sat.

"That's my wife, Rebekah, and my daughter, Emery. You stay one hundred paces from her at all times and we'll be just fine," Chiron said, advancing a step.

Hale held up his hands. "Just wanting to get the lay of the land," he said innocently. I'll stay one hundred paces from her, he thought with a smirk, but I can't promise she'll stay away from me.

There wasn't much to do while the wagons were moving. Walk and stare out at the countryside passing by, walk and eat dust, walk and ignore the blisters on his heels. Aprica looked different on foot than it did whizzing by through a carriage window. The colors bleached in the heat of the sun, the dusky green of sagebrush and the spiky spines of aloe vera blending into a monochromatic haze. The cerulean line of the sea was visible in the distance, but it pulled at his mood like the tide, bringing memories bubbling up of trips drinking sparkling wine on a friend's yacht, that time he tossed Stacia Rostina into the sea over her screams and giggles of protest. If only the Nightingale had made it out of the harbor, they wouldn't be tromping around like peasants, chewing on dirt for lunch.

Speaking of lunch, they didn't even stop as the sun reached its zenith in the sky. Chiron's wife and daughter, and his own mother, who had apparently been taken under their wing, passed out rations and water canteens. "Thank you," he said with a devilish smile as Chiron's daughter handed him two strips of jerky and a hard roll.

She smiled and ducked her head, a dimple appearing in her smooth pale cheek. Gods, was there anything more inviting than a set of dimples?

Hale gripped the jerky in his teeth and pulled and pulled, barely able to manhandle off a bite. "Ugh." He spit the bite into the dirt, where the dog instantly appeared to snap up his ration. "This isn't fit for human consumption." He went to toss the piece over his shoulder, but Cal grabbed it from him.

"We shouldn't waste it. We don't know when we'll get another good meal. You can't be so picky. We're not in Se Caelus anymore."

Hale feigned shock, looking around in a panic. "What? Not in Se Caelus? This is the first I've realized!"

"Will you just stop?" Cal snapped. "Enough. Just for a few hours, can you stop being Hale and be my brother again?" He whirled and stalked back towards their mother, leaving Hale hanging with his mouth open.

By the time Chiron called for the wagons to pull off the road into a stand of scraggly trees, Hale was ready to drop from exhaustion. It was only sheer stubbornness that had stopped him from asking if they were there yet a thousand times. His feet ached, his legs ached, his hips ached, his back ached. The skin on his face and neck was tight and sunburned, despite his normally tan complexion. The number of chores needed to ready the caravan for camp was mindboggling. Unhitch the horses. Comb the horses, feed the horses, water the horses. Who knew horses were so damn needy? Gather wood, start a fire, carry water to set it for boiling. To put it mildly, he was in hell. This was hell. Not even the sight of Emery chopping vegetables on the side of her wagon raised his flagging spirits. Who had time to care about girls when they were this tired? Not to mention hungry. His stomach was a yawning chasm of emptiness. He had half a mind to try to seduce the potatoes going in Emery's pot; at this moment, they looked far more attractive than the girl herself.

"Hale?" Brea appeared at his side, Cal in tow. "Can I talk to you boys for a moment? Sim Chiron said I can borrow you while dinner is cooking."

"He doesn't want us to build him a palace or something before we eat?" Hale asked, but then he caught Cal's eye and fell silent. "Sure."

The fading twilight cast shadows of knotty pines as Brea led them into a little clearing under a massive carob tree. Seed pods littered the hard ground and crunched under Hale's boots. She turned, her eyes shining with tears. "I thought we should take a moment. To say goodbye to your father. I hate that he won't be laid to rest with the other Firena ancestors in their tomb in Greenhelm Park…but nothing is how it's supposed to be. At least we can give him a sendoff. Help ease his passing."

Hale swallowed, his throat dry. His eyes were drier. He didn't think he could summon tears for his father's passing. One more failure. He had never been enough son for his father, but at least he could be here for his mother. "It's a great idea, Mother. What would you like to do?"

"I was thinking we could each say a few words, and then…sing a song, perhaps."

"I'll start," Cal said, shrugging his shoulders.

Brea smiled, her face lighting up. "Go ahead, darling."

"I was thinking today about all the times up at the lake house. Just how different he seemed there. It was the only time I felt like he could really…let go. The only time I would see him without his waistcoat, reading the paper with his sleeves rolled up in the morning…" Cal began to recount his memories of their summers at the lake house, a stately home that had been in his father's family for generations. Hale had fond memories of the lake house as well, but mostly when his father wasn't there. He combed through his memories, desperately searching for a memory of his father that wasn't filled with tension and taut breath, his father's dark disapproval, lectures about what it took to honor the Firena legacy. Honoring the Firena legacy, he had learned at a young age, did not include enjoying any of life's pleasures. It meant duty and responsibility. Work and achievement. Not humor or play or fun. Those did not honor the Firena legacy.

"Hale?" Brea was looking at him with anticipation. Hale started, realizing Cal had finished. Hale cleared his dry throat. "I was thinking about that harvest festival the year after you opened the winery. You and Father hosted that party in the vineyard, and the King came, and all the ministers. Father had bought you those ruby earrings—"

"He said they'd match the wine in my glass…" Brea finished, with a little laugh.

"Right," Hale said. "He wouldn't shut up about how you'd negotiated all the contracts and sourced the best grapes and set it up…He was so proud of you. He was chewing everyone's ear off. That night…we felt like a family."

Brea nodded, the sadness in her eyes tempered by her wistful smile. "Thank you, Hale."

"What's your story, Mother?" Cal asked.

"Have I ever told you the story of how your father courted me?"

The boys shook their heads.

"Well. You know your father is a tenacious man when he sees something he wants. I was nearly engaged to another man, a patrician's son I'd known since childhood. I was at the ranch and your father and uncle came in to look at a stallion. He insisted that your uncle wait at the stable and check out some other options while he put this stallion through its paces. He got out in the paddock with the horse, and before

I knew it, he was leaping the fence and galloping away across the countryside!"

"He stole a horse?" Cal asked.

Brea held up her hand. "I was outraged. I looked at your uncle, who only shrugged and said I better go after him. I hopped on my horse and took off. I was ready to chew his ear off, to call the constable, to do something! I finally found him on a path next to a nearby lake. I flew off my horse ready to give him a piece of my mind, and he dropped to his knees and begged my forgiveness. He said it was the only way he could get me alone. He said he wouldn't go back until I spent the day with him, and after that, if I never wanted to see him again, he'd pay double for the horse and be out of my life."

"So he stole a horse and kidnapped you?" Hale said.

Brea rolled her eyes. "He had this devilish grin on his face, and he was so handsome. I knew right there I was lost. He was so alive back then. You remind me a lot of him, Hale—how he was back then."

"Me?" Hale asked with surprise.

"He was only hard on you because he saw so much of himself in you," she said quietly. She opened her arms and Cal and Hale moved into her embrace automatically, the gesture wired in from childhood. "He loved both you boys." Hale wrapped his arm around his mother's small frame, burying his head in her shoulder, trying to banish the unease her comment had left in him. He wasn't anything like his father, was he? Was that the man he was destined to become?

Brea released them and pulled a small pocket knife from the pouch on her belt. She began carving in the trunk of the tree, a crude rendering of WJF, his father's initials. It was such a small marker to represent a man who Hale had spent his whole life molding himself around.

When she was finished, Brea began to sing, her soprano voice clear and haunting, far too fine for the setting. It was a hymn of the Sower, one of their gods, who supposedly harvested souls ready to move on to more fertile lands.

"Once was a time to sow
Is now a time to reap
To pull the flaxen chaff
From the fields of wheat

Memories are borne
On the fertile sea
Souls of ones we loved
Gone on to find their peace."

The hairs on the back of Hale's neck rose as the last note of his mother's song hung in the air. The sun had dipped below the horizon, and before Hale was only darkness. He took his mother's hand, clinging to it as if she were the only solid thing in this world.

CHAPTER 8

A tempting smell greeted them when they rejoined the other members of the caravan around the fire. The fairer of the two workers—Hale had already forgotten his name—had pulled out a guitar and was strumming it softly. Someone had dragged some logs up around the fire, and Hale took a seat on one next to Griff. Gods, the thing was uncomfortable. Cal sat beside him while Brea went to sit next to Chiron. Emery was stirring the stew, her blonde hair glinting rose gold in the firelight. She really was quite lovely with her round, cherubic face, wide eyes, and long, dark lashes.

"No need to be so obvious," Griff remarked under his breath. "Don't want Chiron to cut you in your sleep."

"I don't know what you're talking about," Hale said. "I'm staring at the voluptuous curves of that stew pot."

Cal snorted, leaning forward. "I wouldn't waste your breath, Griff. Trying to get Hale to give up admiring women is like trying to tame the wind. But with more bluster."

Griff laughed. "Appreciate the warning."

"I'm glad you two can bond at my expense. You're very welcome—" But all thoughts of his companions were lost when a hot bowl of soup and a crusty brown roll were shoved into his hands. He flashed his best smile, only to find that Chiron's wife was on the receiving end. Ah, well. Wouldn't hurt to ingratiate himself with her, too. Older women loved him just as much as young ones.

"Don't suppose you have any ale?" he called after her. She didn't respond.

"Guess that's a *no*," he murmured, digging in to dinner. The stew wasn't bad—sure, it was no lamb shank drizzled with mint juice, but it filled him with warmth and quieted the gnawing emptiness in his belly.

"Sim Chiron," his mother said after taking a demure bite of her own stew. "How did you find yourself running this caravan? You're an army man, if I'm not mistaken?"

"You've a keen eye, madam," Chiron said. "Served for twenty years. Spent a lot of my time on border patrol, or on loan to Tamros. Bandits have been growing increasingly bold in the past ten years as the Tamrosi government has fallen into infighting and squabbles. There's not enough money to pay soldiers to patrol, and not enough will to make it happen."

"Aprica volunteered its soldiers? That seems unusually...charitable of King Vespian."

"It came at a price. Favorable terms for Tamrosi timber, hops, grapes—whatever the Aprican elite wanted. It didn't work, though. The forests in Tamros are so thick, the bandits can hide in there for years. They've even set up a town in the foothills of Mount Elkri—it's a hell of a place, a den of thieves, slavers, and murderers—home base for their raiding parties, where they can steal from whoever comes their way. They've even taken to raiding into southern Aprica."

"A town of bandits? How come I've never heard of it?" Hale asked.

Captain Brimmer chimed in from across the fire. "Sryalta is no subject for civilized conversation. No place for civilized folk, neither."

"Why doesn't the government wipe this town from the map?" Brea murmured.

"We tried," said Chiron. "It was an epic failure. We...I...lost many men. If they don't want you coming, you ain't getting in. And if they don't want you leaving..." Chiron heaved a sigh. "The kings were talking about making another go at the town, but it would have been suicide. Not without a much larger force than we were willing to commit."

Brea softened. "Is that why you left the army?"

Chiron shrugged his massive shoulders. "Yes and no. I kind of fell into this role. Me and my men escorted a number of caravans through Tamros. I got to know one man well. He was looking to retire, to find someone to sell to. I was looking to make a change. It worked out."

"And your family doesn't mind living on the road?"

"It was better than me being on the road and never seeing them. As long as we're together." Chiron reached out and snaked his arm around his wife's waist, pulling her into a sideways hug. It was strange to see a married couple that was affectionate. Hale didn't think he had ever seen his parents touch each other for years, except when they'd been required to at official functions. He had assumed all married couples were as unhappy.

"Are these bandits still a problem?" Cal called out across the fire. "Will we need to be on alert?"

"Yes," Chiron said. "We'll set a watch each night. You two will join the rotation. There's a lot of territory out there, far from where official forces can help. But don't worry. We've taken this route many times without a problem."

Watch? Hale groaned inside. Hardly any food, hardly any sleep… He'd be half-dead by the time they reached Tamros. He stood and stretched his legs, taking his bowl over to the farthest wagon, where Emery was doing something at a little table.

"Just set your bowl on the bench." She motioned with her head. "We'll wash them later."

"Thank you. The stew was delicious," he said.

She pursed her lips. "I'm sure you've had much finer fare."

"Sometimes the simple pleasures are underappreciated," Hale said, his voice as soft as honey. His eyes were on Emery, but he was getting distracted by her hands.

"What are you doing?" he asked, peering closer through the light of the lantern.

"I'm cutting this caramel and wrapping it," she said. She had a rolling cutter in her hand and was making long slices on a sheet of golden candy.

"Did you make this?" Hale asked, leaning down to examine it more closely in the lamplight.

"Yes," she said. "It's a hobby of mine. Father endures it because I can actually sell it for a pretty penny in Terrasia. I made this batch at the inn this morning, and it's all cooled now and ready to be wrapped."

"Can I try a piece?" Hale asked. He wasn't sure the last time he'd had caramel. There was something quaint about it. It reminded him of happier times. Younger days.

"One," she said. "One of the ugly bits on the end."

"Oh, all I deserve is the ugly bit?"

"Unless you're paying." She giggled.

"Fair point." Hale swooped up one of the jagged edges of one of her rows and popped it in his mouth. The chewiness yielded flavors of buttery toffee and smooth milkiness, but there was something else, too. The bitter bite of coffee and…an earthiness he couldn't place.

"What's in this?"

"It's a coffee stout caramel." She smiled. Those dimples again. Scrumptious.

"You put coffee and beer in this candy?" Hale's eyes widened. "I think I'm in love!"

Even in the low lamplight, Hale could see the blush rising on the round apples of her cheeks. "It's my own recipe. One of my bestsellers."

"It's genius! I never knew candy could be more than boring old chocolate or peppermint."

"There's no end to the flavor combinations you can try! You can add liquor, or herbs, or spices—all sorts of things people wouldn't expect." Her smile turned mischievous. "Now, are you going to stand there, or are you going to help me wrap these up?" Emery had already begun rolling and twisting the caramels in little wax papers.

"Apologies, my lady. I did promise to provide labor on this trip. Let's wrap."

Hale fell into an easy rhythm next to Emery, his mind quieting for the first time in a long time. Somehow he didn't even feel like charming her with witty banter—it was nice to just stand in the glow of her presence, taking in her scent of sugar and lavender.

They were just finishing the last few caramels when Sim Chiron stormed over like a thundercloud. "What did I tell you about getting near my daughter, boy?"

Hale turned to meet his gaze, eye to eye. It was often convenient to be six and a half feet tall. "I meant no disrespect. I was helping the young lady with her labor."

"Father." Emery laid a hand on her father's arm. "He was acting like a perfect gentleman. Don't embarrass me."

Chiron's jaw worked as he looked between Emery and Hale. "You'll take first watch, boy. Come with me now."

Hale inclined his head in a nod as Chiron whirled to stomp back to the fire. Hale flourished a little bow at Emery, and she giggled behind her hand. "I take my leave, my lady," he said, flashing his most heart-stopping grin before turning to follow Chiron. Yes, that one would be putty in his hands.

It turned out watch was Chiron's devilish punishment for Hale's disregard of his order. It apparently involved standing in the cold away from the fire while everyone else got to sleep. "You hear so much as a jackrabbit, you wake me. You hear? We're not far from Se Caelus, but in these times of turmoil, there's no telling who might be out there looking to take advantage."

"So I just...stand out here? For how long?" Hale asked in dismay as the man handed him a sheathed sword and belt.

"Till the moon hits about there." The man pointed to a spot in the sky a ways above the horizon. "Then you wake Stiv."

"Okay," Hale said with more gusto then he felt. Chiron began walking back to the fire. "Which one is Stiv?"

Chiron shook his head. "The burly one," he replied without turning.

Hale glared at his retreating figure, buckling the sword belt around his waist and pulling his cloak closed around him. At least the man had allowed him to retrieve it from his pack. Otherwise, he would probably freeze to death out here and the whole caravan would get robbed by wolves or eaten by bandits. Or the other way around. Hale's mind was growing foggy. The last endorphins from the day had worn off and he was weary to the bone. Not to mention already hungry again. Was this what it was like to be a normal man—like a farmer? Every day, working your fingers to the bone, out in the cold, never enough to eat? Hardly even a life worth living. No wonder peasants died so young. Was that what his life was destined to be now?

They hadn't had time to talk about what the plan was once they got to Terrasia. Perhaps his mother would have contacts who could get them set up there. If not…how many gems did she have in that little pouch of hers? Would it be enough to buy them a house…? Would his mother try to find a winery to work at or manage? She had skills, but what would he and Cal do? They knew nothing about Tamrosi politics; surely, they couldn't continue their father's dream of following in his political footsteps. He would have to…find a trade? Work for a living? The thought made him want to weep. What skills did he have besides seducing women and gambling? Perhaps he could make a living through those two pastimes somehow. Certainly he could win them some money gambling; he had an uncanny luck. Yes, that would do it. He would win his wages gambling and provide a comfortable life for his family. He blew out a sigh, followed by a little chuckle. Work for a living. Ha.

Hale shifted in his boots, wiggling his numb toes, staring out into the darkness. The moon had risen about halfway to the spot it was supposed to reach before he could wake Stiv. He looked back at the camp. The fire was just embers. Everyone had gone to bed. He looked back out into the lonely darkness. Honestly. This watch thing was ridiculous. He held up his hands and blew in them, trying to warm them. How could they expect him to see anything out in this darkness? He should go back to the fire. No one would be the wiser, and he'd just as easily see someone coming there as from here.

Resolved, Hale whirled to head back to the campfire. It was this sentiment that saved him. For when the thrusting jab came, seeking the soft flesh where his belly had been, it found only air.

CHAPTER 9

Hale wasn't sure who was more surprised—him or the man who had attacked him from behind. Hale barreled into the man, his feet tangling with his attacker's. They both went down. Hale landing with a thump on top of the grizzled man. "Bandits!" Hale bellowed. "Attack!"

"Shut up, you dog," another man snarled, hauling Hale off the first man and smashing Hale across the head with his gauntleted fist. Pain exploded through Hale's temple as he fell back to the ground, his vision blurring until four men stood before him instead of two. The metallic sting of blood filled his mouth and visions of his untimely death filled his mind. Thankfully, the attackers soon had more pressing matters to attend to. The rest of the camp had sprung to life, and Chiron was now running at them with bared teeth and bared steel.

The sounds of combat filled the night as Chiron crashed into the men with a bellow. Through his hazy vision and sluggish thoughts, Hale counted more bandits—as many as ten. From the ringing of steel and muffled curses, Hale couldn't tell who was winning. He tried to stand, but his legs didn't seem to be working right. He fell back to his knees, retching onto the dark earth. He had never felt pain like this. It roared in his head, threatening to consume him. He tried to fend it off, to claw past it and reach a coherent thought. Mother. Cal.

Hale crawled across the ground, past the silhouettes of battle backlit by the embers of the fire, the quicksilver of the moon. One man fell with a crash, pierced through—Hale wasn't sure if it was a bandit or one of theirs. He saw faces huddled behind a wagon, female faces—Emery, there…his mother. "Cal," he rasped.

"Help him!" His mother's voice cut through the pain, and Hale whirled, regretting the sudden movement when it was rewarded with an explosion of fire in his temples. Cal was fighting a skinny bandit, swords flashing and clanging in rapid tempo. He and Cal had rudimentary training in fencing, but this—this was different. This was real. A defeat was not just a tick on the breastplate, it was the end. The bandit seemed to have Cal on the defensive, backing towards the wagons while the horses whinnied in fear. Hale summoned whatever strength he had from some hidden well and with a roar ran at the bandit, tackling him at the waist, bearing him to the ground. He punched the man in the face with a savage blow, then again, then again until his fist was bloody and the man's face was barely recognizable.

"Hale!" Cal said. "You got him. The others."

Cal extended his hand to Hale to help him off the ground, and Hale took it gratefully with his own blood-slicked hand. As he went to pull himself up, Cal's eyes shot open with fear and pain and he let out a gurgling gasp.

"Cal!" Hale gasped in horror as he registered the blade protruding from Cal's stomach. It slid out with a sickening suck and Cal fell forwards into his arms, revealing the bandit behind him who had pierced him through with a short sword. Hale collapsed, bearing Cal's weight with him, before rolling him gently onto the ground. Hale was numb. Cold. Unable to think—to speak. The pounding in his head dulled to an ache as the cry of his heart filled his whole being. Cal. Not Cal. Not his brother. No, no, no. They could fix this.

Cal coughed, crimson blood spattering his lips. "Hale." He gasped.

"I'm here." Hale cradled Cal's head in his lap as he took off his cloak and balled it up, pressing it against Cal's wound. There was so much blood—the bandit had pierced him all the way through. Even with the best medical care, it was a grievous wound. And out here…Hale looked around for help but knew there was none. The other men had fallen— Sim Chiron…Stiv…whatever the other man's name was. All down, drowning in pools of their own blood. Captain Brimmer was writhing on the ground, his tricorne hat crushed in the dirt beside him. Griff was nowhere to be seen.

"Mother." Cal coughed again. "Protect Mother."

The bandits were dragging the women out from under the caravan now, and Hale's vision turned red—narrowing to a pinprick. A man with his grubby fist around Brea's upper arm dragged her across the dirt towards the fire.

Hale stood with a roar, grabbing Cal's sword from his blood-soaked hand and tearing across the clearing towards his mother. A bandit stood to meet him and he smashed aside the man's sword with a powerful blow before burying his blade halfway through the man's neck. The man slid to a crumpled heap and the next man came at him, two short swords at the ready. It was the man who had stabbed Cal—the bastard's ugly face had been burned in Hale's memory. Hale parried two blows and kicked the other man in the chest, knocking him back into the dust. The man rolled to scramble out of the way but Hale was too fast, the purifying fire of vengeance searing his blood, burning away the fog. With both hands he buried his sword in the man's back, cutting through him, watering the earth with the man's blood. A grim smile crossed his face as he saw that the blow mirrored the one the man had given Cal. Hale stepped over the man's corpse into a fighting stance, looking for his next fight.

"Stop!" A deep voice rang out clear and strong.

Hale froze.

A tall, dark-haired bearded man held a knife to Brea's throat, his hand tangled in her flaxen hair.

Hale growled, stepping forward. The man stood his ground, tightening his grip. Brea let out a little cry of pain.

"One more step and this woman dies."

"Don't do anything rash," Hale said, his voice rasping like gravel.

"Drop your sword," the man replied. "On your knees."

Hale complied, never breaking eye contact with the man. The smallest slip of that blade…and his mother would be gone. He couldn't risk it.

"Bind him," the man instructed the other bandits, who rushed to Hale's side, painfully twisting leather straps around his ankles and hands. "Tightly." When the men were done, one of the bandits kicked Hale between his shoulder blades, and he toppled forward into the dust.

The bearded man shoved Brea towards another man, who tied her arms and feet. They did the same with Emery and her mother, who was sobbing quietly. The heels of his boots crunched in the dirt as he knelt down, looking into Hale's eyes. "You've got fight in you." Hale looked up and spit into the man's face.

The man stood with a laugh.

"Should we take him?" one of the other bandits asked.

"No," the leader said, walking back to survey the three women before him. "I've seen this kind before. Too much trouble. Let's leave him here for the vultures. Let him contemplate his failures before he dies. Let him think on all the things we will do to this lovely woman. His…mother, I presume?" The man tucked a lock of Brea's hair behind one of her ears.

"Don't touch her!" Hale screamed, struggling against the bonds that bit into his wrists and ankles. He flexed against them, trying to break them through sheer strength, but they only cut into his wrists more, adding more pain to the growing list.

The bearded man chuckled. "He would have been great in the fighting ring. But I don't want to deal with his screaming the whole way back. You two, search the wagons and pile anything of value into the front wagon. Add the prisoners. We're taking the pirate too. I recognize him. He has a bounty on his head. You, round up the horses."

The man returned to Hale's side, crouching down once again. "I'll take good care of your mother. Don't you worry."

"I'll find you," Hale said with as much venom as he could muster. "And kill you."

Another deep chuckle. "Ah, the optimism of youth. Save your strength, young fellow. You'll need it when the crows come."

Hale bared his teeth at the man as he stood again, surveying his men while they pillaged the caravan. Hale caught his mother's eye as she was thrown over a man's shoulder like a sack of grain. "Cal!" she said. "Save Cal." Hale turned his head to where his brother lay, heaving shallow rasping breaths. He needed to get to his brother.

Hale rolled, maneuvering himself back up onto his knees. His ankles were so tightly tied, he could barely inch one knee forward, then the other. Twice, he fell forward, dirt mingling with the blood from the wound at his temple, blurring his vision.

The bandits were hitching a team of horses to the wagon now, rounding up the remaining steeds into a long line.

"Hale," Cal rasped when Hale finally reached his side, collapsing onto the ground beside him. His brother looked pale and pallid. "I'm cold."

"We're going to get you all patched up," Hale said. "Do you have a knife?"

"I think I lost it," Cal said with a weak, apologetic smile. "Sorry."

"You have nothing to be sorry for," Hale said, dropping his head back onto the ground. A memory swam to the surface of when he and Cal were young and would sleep in a nest of blankets on the floor of the lake house. Faces turned towards each other, whispering for hours after their parents had gone to bed.

"You hold on, Cal, okay? I'm going to get us out of this. I'll think of something." In the distance, the wagon was starting to move. The dark-haired bandit swung onto his horse and gave Hale a salute before digging his heels into his steed.

A lump rose in Hale's throat, a feeling of panic and fear unlike any he had ever felt. His charms, his smiles, his swagger—none of it mattered a bit out here in the darkness. Being Hale Firena, son of the most prominent minister in Aprica, it was all meaningless. The girls, the gambling, the parties and fun. He would give up any of it—all of it—if he could just save Cal.

Cal's eyelids fluttered shut.

"Cal!" Hale cried, nudging his brother awake. "Don't you leave me. You fight, okay? Don't stop fighting."

"So…tired. Cold."

Hale scooted closer to his brother until their shoulders were touching. "I'll keep you warm. Just don't leave me, okay? Don't leave me alone out here. I need you. I need my brother."

"Sorry…I let them get me. Never could…fight as well as you."

"Cal, you're a great fighter. You'll heal from this and be stronger than ever. You'll even be able to beat me. Just wait."

Cal's eyes shut again. "Glad…you were my brother. Even if…you're an annoying ass sometimes."

Hale choked out half a sob, half a laugh. Tears began to fall. "I'm glad you're my brother too, Cal."

"Take care of Mother." Cal's breath rasped in and out.

"We'll do it together," Hale said. "Firena brothers stick together. Promise me?"

But Cal said nothing at all.

CHAPTER 10

A crow's shrill caw startled Hale awake. The creature had been sitting on his chest and leaped into the air at his movement. "Get out of here!" he cried, his voice little more than a hoarse whisper. His head fell back to the earth, his neck too weak to hold it up. Cal lay next to him, his blue eyes open and vacant, his skin gray. A sob escaped Hale's throat. Cal was dead. First his father, and now his brother. His mother was on her way to a slaver's auction block, and as for him...he squinted into the sun as it peeked over the horizon. He wasn't long for this world. Quite a fall from grace for the Firena family.

Hale rolled onto his other side, ignoring his muscles' cries of pain, the cramps from the tight bonds at his ankles and wrists. He couldn't look at his brother's corpse any longer. Regrets flashed through him, sharp as knives. He should have spent more time with Cal. Done brotherly things. He shouldn't have teased him all the time. Hale squeezed his eyes shut. Gods. He had been merciless. A complete ass of a little brother and Cal had endured it, tolerating Hale's antics with a shrug of his shoulders and a roll of his eyes. He had even defended Hale to their father when the brunt of his anger seemed to fall on Hale.

"Oh, Cal," he whispered. "I didn't deserve you."

Hale lay back, letting tears of misery leak down his face, dripping into his ears. Eventually, his misery for Cal turned inward. How in the hell was he going to get out of this? He was stuck here, tied up like a solstice ham, getting thirstier by the minute. He awkwardly rolled to his knees, squinting into the sun, looking for something—anything—sharp that he could cut his bonds on. There. Next to Sim Chiron's corpse was the man's sword. Hale slumped on his heels for a moment. It was far. All the way on the other side of the clearing, past the firepit. He sighed. Might as well get moving. He wasn't getting any less dead.

Inch by inch, Hale scooted forward, the knees of his trousers tearing on the rocky ground. The crow watched his progress with a cocked head. "What're you looking at?" Hale grumbled, coughing on the dust coating his mouth and throat. He felt weak and woozy—his head had started swimming as soon as he'd gotten himself upright. He probably had a concussion.

Hale was so intent upon the promised land that was Chiron's sword that he didn't notice a figure approaching from the trees. Not until the person was almost upon him. A figure appeared as if out of thin air, and Hale started, falling to his side. Silhouetted by the morning sun, Hale had to squint to take him in. "Griff?" he asked, relief welling in him. "Is that you?"

"Got yourself in quite a pickle, didn't you, Firena?" Griff stood with one hand on his hip, the other holding a horse's reins. A horse. Hale could have wept at the sight.

"Griff, please. Untie me," Hale begged.

Griff stood for a moment longer than Hale was comfortable with before sighing and pulling a knife from his belt. "Hold still." With a quick flick of his wrists, Griff slit the leather bonds. Hale was free. He groaned, collapsing onto the ground, stretching out spread-eagle with a groan. His shoulders burned the worst, and he sat up slowly, rotating his arms in his sockets to bring the life back into them. "Thanks." He pushed to his feet, swaying slightly.

"You don't look so good," Griff said, examining him.

"You don't look like a trunk full of coin yourself," Hale snapped.

Griff bristled, turning. "Just here to grab some supplies. Best of luck to you."

"Wait." Hale held out his hands beseechingly. "Wait. I'm sorry. My brother is dead, my mother is a captive of that bastard bandit, and my head feels like a marching band just walked through it. But please. Maybe we can help each other."

"I'm the one with the horse and the water skin. Not sure what you can offer me."

"It's not safe, traveling on your own. It will be easier with two. I can keep watch, fight if it comes to it."

"Because you did such a great job keeping watch last time?" Griff scoffed.

That stung. "I raised the cry!"

"They were almost on top of us!" Griff said, his tone clipped. "Captain Brimmer had a bounty on his head, and now I have to go to Sryalta to rescue him. Thanks to you."

Hale closed his eyes. It was his fault, wasn't it? It was all his fault. That Cal was dead, that his mother was gone. "Let me help make it right. I need to rescue my mother. You need to rescue the captain. We can travel together. Help each other."

"I don't need your help. You're a spoiled rich ass who won't last two days in the real world."

Hale weighed his options. He needed that horse. He could try to take it, but Griff struck him as surprisingly scrappy. The lad was the only one who had escaped the bandits unscathed. He needed the boy's help. He looked back at Cal's body, biting his lip. Being Hale wasn't working very well for him in the real world, as Griff had so aptly noted. What would his brother do?

"Please," Hale said. "Griff. I can't change being a spoiled rich ass, but if you help me, I'm your man. If not for me, for my mother. She doesn't deserve whatever those monsters are going to do to her. She's all I have left. Please. Let me help you rescue them. Don't leave me here."

Griff chewed on the inside of his cheek, his eyes narrowed. "If I help you—"

"Thank you, Griff. Thank you, thank you!"

Griff held up his hands. "*If* I help you. I'm in charge. You do what I say when I say it. None of that attitude I saw on the ship. You hear?"

"Whatever you say goes. I swear it." Hale would have promised his left arm if it meant getting on that horse.

Griff heaved a sigh. "I have a feeling I'm going to regret this. But fine. You can come."

Hale pulled Griff into a hug, crushing the smaller boy to his chest. "Thank you."

"Air!" came Griff's muffled voice.

Hale released the boy, stepping back. "Do you have any water?" Hale asked.

Griff rolled his eyes and tossed his waterskin to Hale. "I'm going to search the wagons for provisions."

Hale, after taking a long drink, looked back at Cal. "Do we have time to bury my brother?"

Griff softened and nodded. "There's a shovel in the back wagon. But be quick about it."

Hale buried Cal beneath the carob tree where they had honored his father just last night. It seemed an eternity ago that the three of them had stood, exchanging stories, listening to his mother's clear voice ring out between the pines. Tears dripped down his nose as he tossed the last shovelful of earth over Cal's grave. He stood for a long moment, his thoughts numb, his body aching and protesting from the punishment it had been through.

Hale finally spoke. "Don't know what to say. Except I'm sorry. For all of it. I'll find Mother. I'll keep her safe and be as good a son as you were. Because that's what you'd want me to do."

Hale took a knife he had snagged from one of the bandits' bodies and stepped forward, carving into the tree trunk. The wood was hard and thick, and so he scratched Cal's initials next to his father's. WJF and CAF. With that, he turned, walking back towards the lonely wagons to the task of burying the rest of the men.

Hale found he didn't have much to say over these mens' graves, but he didn't complain about the mess of blisters on his hands, or the work.

He figured that, together with the burial, was something.

"I found a few more waterskins," Griff said when he was done, sorting through a little pile she had made on the ground. "Some good provisions. Dried meat, cheese, oats for the horse. Chiron had some clothes in there if you want to change…his stuff should fit you."

Hale looked down at his clothes, bloody and torn. He nodded woodenly, rinsing the blood off of his face before making his way into the covered wagon to change. He stripped down to nothing, hissing as fabric separated from raw parts. He put on a set of Chiron's clothes— pants, shirt and leather vest, jacket, and a wide-brimmed hat. All around the wagon were signs of the inhabitants. Strings of Emery's lace ribbon tied to the slats above her bedroll, dried flowers in a little jar. A paper bag full of the caramels that he had helped her roll. He reached out and grabbed them before hopping out of the wagon. He pulled Chiron's sword belt off his body, re-sheathing the sword at his hip. A smaller sheath on the other side of the belt held a dagger.

"Ready?" Griff asked. He had filled the horse's saddlebags to bursting with their provisions; Hale had to wedge in the bag of caramels.

"I'm ready," Hale said.

"You're bigger than me," Griff said, pursing his lips. "You take the saddle. I'll sit in front."

The old Hale would have cracked a joke at that, but Hale simply nodded, swinging gracefully into the saddle. He leaned down and offered his hand, helping Griff scramble up in front of him. The lad weighed as much as a feather pillow.

Griff took the reins, and without a backward glance, kicked the horse forward.

Hale did look back, saying a silent goodbye and thank you to Chiron, Stiv, and the other men who had lost their lives. Hale looked down at himself as they rode past—bloodied and dirty, wearing a dead man's clothing. And grateful for it. He felt something shift inside him. Harden. Griff was right—the old Hale wouldn't have lasted two days in the real world. But that Hale had died—had been buried alongside Cal. This new Hale might stand a fighting chance.

CHAPTER 11

As it turned out, the journey to Sryalta wasn't the problem. It was getting in.

Hale's uneasy alliance with Griff held for the two-day journey. The boy was about as talkative as a stump, but he had been to Sryalta before—that much was clear. He directed their horse with sure knees. When Hale mustered the energy to attempt a plan, shoving aside the looming specter of his brother's death and the physical depravities likely being visited on his mother at this very moment, Griff rejected every one of Hale's suggestions.

"Sryalta isn't a city you enter unnoticed," Griff said over breakfast, drawing a rough map in the dirt with a stick. "The only entrance is through a narrow pass between two cliffs. The city is built into the hillsides and the base of the cliffs between the gorge." They had made camp at the foothills, where the mountains started to rise, to the east of the entrance Griff spoke of.

"Stupid place for a bandit to build a city. No way out if the army comes."

"Well, yes, but first they'd have to get in through the canyon. And they never have."

"Remind me again why we can't just walk through the front door?"

"We could, if we wanted to be arrested and sold as slaves. I'm not too keen on that myself."

"I'm open to suggestions," Hale said with a sigh, unwrapping a caramel from the little brown sack in the saddlebags. He had eaten half the bag in the last two days.

"How can you eat candy for breakfast?" Griff stuck his tongue out with an expression of disgust.

Hale shrugged. "Makes me feel better. My sugar habit is the least of our concerns right now. How the hell are we going to get in?" Not to mention getting out. He couldn't even begin to worry about that little problem.

"There is a way I know of. It's...harrowing, to say the least."

"My favorite kind of entrance."

"How are you at climbing?"

"Griff, I'm a picture of physical perfection. There's very little this body can't do." Hale attempted a wry grin. There was a grain of truth to his boast. Even as a boy, he'd always been able to tackle all sorts of physical challenges. Whatever else the Sower had given him, he was gifted with uncanny reflexes, aim, and endurance.

"So...never climbed before?"

"How hard can it be?"

Griff let out a grunt. "Assuming the weight of your ego doesn't drag you down the cliffside...pretty hard. But I don't see another way."

"Is that how you got out last time?"

Griff's head shot up. "What did you say?"

"It's pretty obvious. Your face turns white every time we mention it."

"I don't want to talk about that. Drop it."

Hale held up his hands. "You're the boss. But whatever you can tell me about the city...it could make a difference. If things go sideways in there."

Silence. Followed by a heavy sigh. "I escaped…that place. I made it out, but I didn't have any supplies… I was on my last breath out here. Right around here, probably. Captain found me. Coulda turned me in, but he made me a member of his crew. Swore I'd never go back. But I can't just leave him." Griff's smooth face was as hard as stone.

"What'd the captain do? To get the bounty on his head."

"Raided another vessel, fair and square. Turned out to belong to some Alesian merchant who takes himself way too seriously."

"What'll they do with him?"

"Turn him over to the merchant. Who'll probably have him executed."

"What will they do to my mother?" Hale asked, the words soft.

Griff swirled a pattern in the dirt with his stick, not meeting Hale's eye. "Fine lady like that, they probably won't rough her up too bad. Sell her to some perverted old lord or earl to be his personal plaything."

Disgusting. An image surfaced in Hale's mind, unbidden—Sim Daemastra bowing over his mother's hand, his too-tight skin stretching back from his lecherous smile. The soldier had said that the man wanted his mother. Surely his reach couldn't extend so far? Was it possible the bandits' attack was not as random as they had thought?

"Do you know where the bandit might be keeping them?"

"He probably already sold them to Sim Rakoni. He's the slaver who owns Sryalta's auction house. He handles all the sales."

"Have you met this Rakoni?"

"Yes. He's a bastard, but a civilized bastard. He loves nice clothes, expensive food, and wine. The auction house is designed like a fancy brothel or something, with booths for patrons, private back rooms, gambling…"

"Gambling?" Hale perked up. That was a useful tidbit.

"He runs the fighting arena too. Takes all the bets on the fighting champions."

Hale popped another caramel in his mouth, savoring the smooth flavors of coffee and beer mingling with the caramel itself. A man of refined taste. There had to be something there they could use. A play…a gamble to win his mother's freedom. And the captain, he amended.

"Need a minute before we go," Griff said, standing and stretching, heading towards a boulder a few yards away.

Hale stood, dusting off his trousers. He swallowed a dig about Griff's strange shyness. The boy hadn't taken a piss in front of Hale in the two days they'd traveled together. He sighed. The old Hale might have made a comment, but not the new Hale. Whatever Griff did behind boulders was Griff's business.

"We should get a move on," Griff said, reappearing. "It'll take the better part of the day to hike up to where we can start to climb down into the ravine behind the city."

"Hike?" Hale asked. "We're not taking the horse?"

"Too obvious. We'll tie him up in those trees where he's relatively hidden. We go on foot."

On foot. Hale suppressed a shudder. Were there any two worse words?

Griff set a punishing pace up the mountainside. The air smelled earthy and sharp from scrubby underbrush that grasped at his trousers as they passed. The sky was a cloudless blue, the same pure azure that used to paint the backdrop of his perfect life. Now, it seemed to mock him. Where were the gray storm clouds and tempestuous rain that matched his current predicament? Up, up, up they climbed, but Hale's mood foundered, sinking low. Surely, he could have done something differently back in the camp—could have fought harder, not left his brother's side. He'd been standing watch. If he'd been more vigilant, the camp would have had more time. Chiron and his men could have gotten the women to safety. A thousand scenarios played out in his head, a thousand ways he could have turned the tide, done one thing different to stop that sword from piercing his brother through. He wasn't used to these feelings. Regret. Guilt. They were gnawing parasites, eating him from the inside out. What would be left of him when they were finished? He wasn't sure he could bring himself to care.

Griff slowed down before him, his hands on his hips, blowing out a long breath. "We're close to the top. We'll be able to see the town once we're over the edge, and in theory, they could see us if anyone was looking close enough. Try not to...do anything stupid."

Hale's brows drew together. "What stupid thing are you referring to?"

"I don't even know," Griff said. "I'm sure you could come up with something if left to your own devices. Don't…start a rockslide, or holler at the wind, or anything."

Hale pressed a finger to his lip in mock confusion. "So when we're sneaking into the city, I *shouldn't* do anything to obviously announce our presence? Is that right? This is all so new and strange."

Griff scowled. "Just…follow me."

"Thanks for the vote of confidence," Hale muttered under his breath.

Hale scrambled up the steep incline after Griff, rocks and dirt giving way beneath his feet. When he reached the summit of the ridge, it took him a moment to steady himself. They could see for miles from their new perch—north across the plains that stretched towards Se Caelus, west to the shining ribbon of the sea. And before them, a bustling metropolis of rock-hewn buildings, colorful tents, and narrow corridors.

Hale gawked at the sight, trying to calculate how many people actually lived here.

"Thousands," Griff said, as if Hale had spoken his question out loud. "Thousands of the worst types of lowlives and thieves. Trust no one. Talk to no one. Keep your head down. You're conspicuous enough, but no need to be challenging every man we pass to a fight with your eyes."

Hale opened his mouth in affront.

"Don't." Griff held up a hand. "I'm going to go down first. You follow me precisely. If you fall, try not to fall on me, will you?"

Oh, yes. The climb. With a knot in his throat, Hale looked over the edge. It had to be several hundred feet of sheer rock, punctuated only by little jagged outcroppings and knobby bushes growing at impossible angles. "We're climbing…down that?"

"How hard can it be?" Griff smirked before lowering himself over the edge.

Hale took a deep breath in. An adventure. Just another adventure. Beating the odds. He was good at that. He just had to beat these odds too.

The climb wasn't as bad as Hale expected. Sure, his fingernails were bloody nubs, sweat poured buckets into his eyes and down his ass-crack, and his muscles ached and cramped, but they were making steady progress. The cliff face was surprisingly sturdy—he'd only sent a few rocks tumbling down towards Griff when he tried to grab onto them. He tried not to look down but had to from time to time to find an appropriate foothold. About fifty feet above the roofs of the first houses, the cliff face jutted out into a little ledge about a foot wide. It was here that he caught up with Griff, putting a shaking foot on the ledge, laying his face against the rock as he let his arms hang limp.

"Well…that sucked," he finally said, turning to face Griff.

The lad's face was pale and sweaty, his chest heaving. "For once, I agree with you."

"What's the plan once we get in there?"

Griff looked down with a shrug, examining his bloody fingernails. "Not sure."

Hale narrowed his eyes. "You've been cagey the whole ride. You know what we're going to face in here to get them back. You do have a plan, don't you? What are we going to do?"

Griff finally looked up, still not meeting Hale's eyes, gazing at the maze of buildings below them. "I was going to offer a trade."

"A trade?" Hale recoiled.

"Keep your voice down!" Griff cringed. "We're not far from the surface now. We don't want to draw attention."

Hale had gone as cold as ice. The little viper was going to betray him! Trade him for Captain Brimmer. What a fool he'd been, trusting him. He'd tried to act as saintly and meek as Cal for two days and look what it would've gotten him. Well, time for the old Hale to make a reappearance.

Hale grabbed Griff by the front of his shirt, lifting him off the ground. "You trading me to a slaver was not part of our deal."

"Put me down, you stupid ox." Griff grunted, his hands scrambling towards Hale's face, through Hale's arms were far too long. Griff's feet flapped in the open air until one found purchase, kicking Hale directly in the kneecap.

"Ow!" Hale cried, doubling over and dropping Griff back on the ledge, clasping his offended leg. But the motion of leaning over unbalanced him and his heel slipped off the edge of the rock wall. Hale straightened, trying to regain his equilibrium, his arms windmilling, his eyes going wide.

"Hale!" Griff said, reaching for Hale's shirt to haul him back up.

But it was too late. Hale was already falling into open air.

CHAPTER 12

A rotted wooden roof slowed Hale's momentum, but it was a serendipitously-placed bed that broke his fall. *Breathe,* Hale thought when his stunned mind began working again. *Breathe! Air!* His lungs felt like they had collapsed in on themselves. Finally, with a shuddering gasp, he forced blessed air into his body, nearly weeping in relief. He sat up slowly, his pounding head reeling at the movement. After a quick examination, Hale concluded that nothing was broken. He had been lucky.

The house he had crashed into so unceremoniously seemed empty— another stroke of luck. Through the hole in the roof, Griff was visible scrambling down the mountainside after him. He ran around and came bursting through the front door. He sagged in relief when he saw Hale sitting up, his legs over the side of the bed. "Holy hell, man. You should be dead!"

"I got lucky," Hale said with a wheezing cough. "Now stay away from me. We go our separate ways from now on. I'm not letting you hand me over in exchange for the captain."

Griff crossed his arms over his chest and stuck his hip out in that way Hale had come to learn meant—*you're an idiot.* "I was going to turn myself over for the captain, you idiot!"

Hale stood up slowly, a hand to his back as he slowly inched towards Griff. Everything hurt. Even things he didn't know could possibly hurt. "You were going to turn yourself over? That's your grand plan?"

Griff shrugged. "It's the only bargaining chip I have. It's impossible to break anyone out of this town. You'll see. This is the only way."

"And why would this slaver even agree to take you in exchange for Captain Brimmer? Isn't there a bounty on his head? You're..." Hale paused, swallowing the word "nobody."

"I have to at least try, all right?" Griff's voice cracked.

"All right, I'm sorry. I don't think trading yourself for the captain is the answer. He wouldn't want that. He got you out of here, right?"

"If my plan is so terrible, I'm open to suggestions. But we should get the hell out of here. If someone heard you fall, they'll be here any minute to investigate."

"I do, in fact, have a plan," Hale said, turning his torso tenderly. His back popped in five different places and he sagged in relief. "Lead the way."

Griff wrinkled his nose. "Follow me."

The streets of Sryalta were twisted and dark. Tall, mismatched buildings leaned precariously over the narrow alleyways. The people they passed eyed Hale and Griff with dark eyes full of suspicion, which was fine by Hale, as he couldn't help himself from doing the same. He had never come across a shiftier set of people—scarred, dirty, ugly, bristling with weapons, sporting mismatched clothes. He shuddered. How had he gone from sipping minted bourbon with the King of Aprica to this?

As they made their way from the outskirts into the city center, Hale explained the plan in low tones. "We're going to walk into this slaver's gambling hall and walk out with my mother and Captain Brimmer. Plus a set of horses, provisions, and an escort to Alesia. Easy as pie."

Griff scoffed. "And how are we going to accomplish that?"

"He's going to hand them over."

"Hale. This man is a cutthroat. If the sick bastards of this city were civilized enough for a monarch, he'd be their king. He didn't get that power by giving things away because people ask nicely."

"We're not going to ask nicely. We're going to win it. In a wager."

"You plan to gamble for your mother?"

Hale paused, stepping into the shadow of an alley. "We haven't known each other for very long, so you'll have to take my word for it when I say that I am very, very good at gambling. I'm uncannily lucky. You saw me fall off that cliff! What are the odds I would have fallen into a soft feather bed and not...I don't know, a blacksmith's shop? You're going to have to trust me here."

Doubt was written across Griff's freckled face, but he finally nodded. "What are we going to gamble with?"

Hale rubbed the stubble on his jaw. "That is a better question. We'll have to go in looking like high stakes players—people of importance. We'll need to steal some nice clothes, get a good bath and a shave—though not you, you don't even have one whisker, do you? And steal some money to start playing with."

"You don't rob people in Sryalta. That's a great way to get yourself killed."

"I'm open to suggestions," Hale mimicked.

Griff turned, pacing into the darkness of the alley, kicking a blackened head of cabbage out of his way. He turned back, his eyes troubled.

Hale perked up. "You have an idea, don't you?"

"It's a last resort..."

"I think we're in last resort territory. Don't hold out on me, man!"

"I might know someone who can help us."

"What? You have a contact here? Why didn't you say so?"

"Because I don't...know...that they will be friendly. I didn't leave...on the best of terms."

"Will they slit your throat on sight?"

"No." Griff heaved a sigh.

"Then we're going."

Griff's contact was an innkeeper who kept one of the safer establishments in Sryalta: The Black Boar Inn. They wound their way through town, crossing a large market square filled with colorful tents and even more colorful merchandise. Hale slowed to gawk at the wares: fortunetellers with cards and crystals spread over purple cloths, apothecaries with bottles promising all sorts of impressive results—a powder to grow *what, how* big?

"Come on." Griff grabbed his arm and dragged him past as he tried to peer at the little green bottle.

"The ladies will sing songs about you, my friend!" the merchant called after him.

"This place is amazing," Hale said, some of his disgust turning to awe. "What kind of fruit is this?" He picked up a spiky ball about the size of an apple.

In a blink, he found the fruit replaced with the point of a sword aimed between his eyes. "No sampling the merchandise," the man behind the cart said through the gap in his leering smile.

"Apologies," Hale said, putting the fruit away before backing away hastily and hurrying after Griff. But before he reached him, he caught sight of a bottle in a wine merchant's stall. The label looked familiar. He leaned over the makeshift counter, trying to get a closer look.

"You have fine taste, my friend," the proprietor said. "Wine from one of the finest vineyards in Aprica. They say drinking a bottle takes a year off your life."

Hale's heart did a somersault into his gut. Now he knew why he recognized the label. It was his mother's. To think it had made it this far, that it was being touted as one of the finest vintages in Aprica... Brea would have been beside herself with excitement had the circumstances been different. Who knew where his mother was at that moment, whether she was safe? Even if she was, she'd never be making a bottle like that again.

"Hold on to that one," Hale said. "I have it on good authority that the vintner's retired."

The dark-haired man raised an impressive eyebrow, but before he could reply, Griff returned and tugged Hale along by the bicep.

"You're going to get us killed," Griff said under his breath. "You keep touching things and talking to everyone!"

"Pardon me for talking to someone. I wasn't aware that was a crime."

"In Sryalta, catching the wrong person's attention will get you killed. Stay out of people's notice."

"Easy to do when you're a tiny redhead," Hale muttered. "Less so when you're built like an Aprican god."

"Don't flatter yourself," Griff retorted.

"Demi-god?"

"There's The Black Boar," Griff said, pointing to a three-story building with a cedar shake roof that looked…almost respectable.

"How do you know this person again?"

"It's complicated."

"Better make it uncomplicated. Don't want me screwing things up by saying the wrong thing, right?" Hale flashed his devilish grin.

"Fair point." Griff pursed his lips, making his way down the side of the hotel around the back. "When I here before…I was a slave. To a rich merchant. We came to the tavern here sometimes, and the proprietor, Theo, he kind of…took notice of me. The situation I was in. It was a bad one. My master was…not kind."

Hale furrowed his brow. Took notice?

They rounded the back of the hotel into a small courtyard with a few chairs and a trash bin. A wiry boy in a white apron was straining to tilt a heavy trash can into the larger bin. "Let me help you with that," Hale said, striding across the courtyard and lifting the bin, tilting it effortlessly.

The boy skittered back like a started cockroach, his eyes wide and wary. "Who are ya? What ya doin' 'ere?"

"We're old friends of—" Hale looked at Griff. "Theo. Is he around?"

The boy rubbed the back of his neck, clearly unsure about his next move. "Old friends, ya say?"

"We'd just like to say *hello,*" Griff said, glaring at Hale. "We won't cause any trouble."

The boy nodded, apparently deciding they looked trustworthy enough. "I'll git 'im," he said before disappearing through the back door.

"So, Theo helped you out?" Hale asked.

"He helped me escape. Unfortunately, I was robbed outside of town, and left with nothing. Like I said, I would have been screwed if Captain Brimmer hadn't found me."

"That's great. I don't see why you were so hesitant to see him."

"Theo wanted me to come back. And I didn't."

"Come back—why? It wouldn't be safe for you, right?"

Griff shook his head. "Right. But that was the deal. I promised, in exchange for his help. Once things died down, I'd come back, and…"

"And what?"

Griff looked at Hale with an inscrutable gaze. "There's something more… Something you don't know."

"No shit. What's this all about?"

"I—"

A tall, sturdy man with a thick beard and forearms like clubs appeared in the doorway. On his face was an expression Hale couldn't quite place. Astonishment? Reverence? "As soon as Jay said there was someone asking for me, I knew it was you." The man rushed to stand before Griff, and to Hale's utter amazement, fell on his knees before him, pressing his face into Griff's stomach. "Augustina, I knew you'd come back."

Hale looked from Griff to the man and back to Griff, who had taken off his hat. *Her…*hat. "Augustina?" he asked weakly.

CHAPTER 13

Hale's knees threatened to buckle beneath him. He sank onto a wooden crate. Griff was a girl. He was an idiot for not seeing it. Slight frame, small stature, not a whisker on her face. Traits that Hale had credited to Griff being young were so obvious in retrospect. Always running off to pee behind trees and boulders... He cursed himself. *Stupid.*

Griff was standing, her hands flapping in the air uselessly, her green eyes fixed not on the man who continued to press his cheek to her stomach, but on Hale. Apology was etched across her face. Griff's reticence to talk about her time in Sryalta—her enslavement—suddenly took on new meaning. What kind of horrors had been done to her here, a young girl innocent and beautiful enough to inspire such devotion? Hale found the embers of his anger at Griff quickly dying. Who was he to judge her? He didn't know what her life had been like. It was probably easier to be an unnoticed boy than deal with...this. Hale curled his lip as Theo stood, taking Griff's hand in his own.

"I knew you hadn't betrayed me. Hadn't gone back on our deal,"

Theo said. "I waited for you. I didn't take a wife. There is no one but you."

Wife?

"Can we get inside?" Griff…Augustina…said. "I'll explain everything."

Theo nodded, looking suspiciously back at Hale.

"He's my traveling companion," Griff said quickly. "He helped see me safely here. He's a friend."

Hale offered a friendly smile and stuck out his hand. "Hale."

Theo took his hand after a moment of hesitation. The boyfriend usually didn't like him. He was used to it.

"All right," Theo said. "Come on in. Can I get you two something to eat?"

Hale's grin broadened. "Theo, your words are music to my ears."

The Black Boar was a reputable establishment, at least for a town full of thieves and cutthroats. Tall windows spanned the two-story common room, which was flanked by balconies leading to the upper levels. The room was filled to bursting with patrons enjoying hot stew and cold pints, but Theo managed to snag them two high stools at the bar.

"Venison stew all right?" Theo asked.

"Actually, do you have a juicy flank steak?" Hale asked. "I'm craving—"

"Shoulda clarified. Venison stew's what we got."

Hale closed his mouth and nodded. "Venison stew will be great."

As soon as Theo vanished into the kitchen, Hale turned, giving Griff his best raised eyebrow. "Augustina? Or should I say, my lady?"

Griff's face turned scarlet. "Shut it. I have nothing to apologize for. I learned a long time ago that life's easier when you're a man."

"I'm not disagreeing with you."

Griff continued. "I mean, take you, for instance. You probably would have spent our entire trip trying to sleep with me, had you known I was female."

"Don't flatter yourself, darling. You're not exactly my type." Though now that Hale was really looking, really seeing Griff, he had to admit, there were some appealing parts. Delicate bone structure and hands, a quaint, upturned nose, full, rosy lips…

"I'm quite a vision when I get cleaned up. I wasn't a prize slave because I was good at climbing."

"Wait, are you…mad at me? For saying I wouldn't have hit on you? Do you *want* me to hit on you?"

Griff's face turned even redder. "No, you idiot. I'm just trying to explain—" She broke off as Theo returned with two bowls of stew and dark rolls. "Thank you," she said weakly.

"Don't suppose I can trouble you for a pint?" Hale asked. "I have a fierce hunger."

"Just have a pale ale on tap," Theo said.

"Whatever you got," Hale said.

When Theo put the frosty glass down before him, Hale thought he would weep. When he took his first sip, he closed his eyes with delight, enjoying the cold bite on his tongue. If there was one thing he would say for tragedy and travel, it was that they brought out life's small pleasures in stark relief.

"I'll have one too," Griff said.

"Ah, beer ain't a drink for a lady," Theo said. "I'll see if I have some sherry in the back."

"Do you see what I mean?" Griff said after he had disappeared again. "I can't even get a beer as a woman."

"You can have a sip of mine," Hale passed it over. "But only because I'm a good person who wouldn't have hit on you."

Griff rolled her eyes but took the beer, groaning in pleasure after taking a sip. "Damn, that's good."

"So how long have you been Griff?" Hale asked, motioning at her form.

"Since I left this place. I wanted to learn to sail with the captain, but it's bad luck to have women on board, or so they say. He thought it'd be safer if I was a boy."

"And you don't mind living that way?"

"The captain was my family." Griff tore off a hunk of bread and dipped it in the stew. "Only person who's ever done anything for me without wanting something from me. I'd dress up as a goat if it meant sticking with him. Plus, I love to sail. And I'm damn good at it. Captain thinks my people were sailors from the Centu peninsula. In Alesia."

"You don't know where you're from?"

Griff shook her head. "Grew up in Sryalta. Don't know how I got there. Captain's theory is that my parents' vessel was attacked or sank in a squall. Slavers brought me here."

To not know where one came from... Hale shook his head. He couldn't imagine. "Have you been to Alesia? Investigated?"

"Been there," Griff said around a bite. "This is really good, by the way. Maradis, the capital, is the loveliest place you ever saw. Green trees for days, silhouetted by snowcapped mountains on both sides...and so many islands. Hundreds of 'em. A pirate could hide out there all his life."

"Nowhere's prettier than Aprica," Hale said, his heart twisting. "The beaches and the palm trees..."

"It's a different kind of beautiful. Aprica is pretty on the surface...but Alesia has depth. And good food." She took another bite. "Maybe Captain Brimmer and I will head south when this is all over. It's time to try something new. Plus, I have a bad feeling about this new Aprican government."

"You're not going to stay here and marry Theo?" Hale asked, bringing his hand to his chest in feigned chock.

Griff glared daggers at him and opened her mouth to answer, but at that moment, Theo returned with a glass of golden sherry for Griff.

"Thank you," she said sweetly, but when Theo turned his back, she stuck her tongue out at Hale in a gagging motion. Hale grinned and lifted his beer in a mock toast.

Theo turned back, pushing his sleeves up. "All right. I have a few minutes to talk. Augustina, I want to hear all about where you've been. Why it's taken you so long to return...We only thought it'd take a month or so until the search for you died down." The man wasn't terrible to look at, Hale supposed. Gentle brown eyes, a round nose, that full dark beard. Tall and stocky. Strong. But Hale didn't blame Griff for not wanting this life. It'd be like being married to...a tame brown bear. Hale chuckled to himself, and when Theo looked his way with a glare, he buried his face in a spoonful of stew. Griff was right—it was good. Spicy and warm—fennel and shallots and bits of smoky venison.

Griff was spinning a tale now about wanting to return, but being taken by pirates. According to Griff's wide pleading eyes, it had taken years for Captain Brimmer to find her. It seemed she was doubling down on her betrayal of this man. Hale didn't mind. It seemed unlikely that Theo would help them if Griff told him she never intended to marry him. And they needed his help.

"But now the captain has been taken, and there's a bounty on his head, and I need to make it right, to save him. Hale's mother's been taken as well. We need your help to free them. Consider it a wedding present?" She smiled halfheartedly.

"It's no easy feat, negotiating with the slaver. What do you have to trade?"

"We're not going to trade," Hale said, cutting in. "We're going to win them."

"Win them?"

"Yes. Griff, er, Augustina, explained that this slaver is a gambling man. We need to go in as worthy opponents. Make him a wager he can't refuse. Beat him, and we walk out with my mother and Captain Brimmer. Easy peasy."

"You'd have to have the luck of the gods to beat Rakoni in his own establishment. It can't be done." Theo crossed his burly forearms over his chest.

"Hale's…very good at gambling," Griff said weakly. He could tell she was doubting their mad plan. "He thinks it can work. We have to try."

"We need to get cleaned up, put on some nice clothes, and get a little coin to get me started," Hale said. "I'll do the rest. Before you know it, the fair Augustina will be back here in your arms forevermore."

Griff glared at Hale, who flashed a wide grin at the innkeeper. Theo scratched his beard. "I guess I can find you something…it still seems terribly dangerous. Augustina, I'm not sure I like this."

"Please. It's the last favor I'll ask of you before…we wed," Griff said, half-choking on the words.

Theo grinned, displaying a prominent hole where an incisor should have been. He took Griff's hand and kissed it over the bar. "I'll make the arrangements. I'll get you two rooms so you can get cleaned up." He turned, heading through the swinging door to the bowels of the inn.

"I'm an extra large," Hale called after him. "Get me something in purple velvet, if you can!"

Griff slouched, letting her head thunk forward on the bar. "The Huntress take me now; I'm headed straight to hell."

"Don't forget—hell's where all the fun happens. And seriously, don't kill yourself over it. It'd be like being married to…" Hale was still trying to figure out what animal Theo reminded him of. Not really a bear… "A kindly buffalo!" he finished triumphantly. "If he's foolish enough to trust you a second time, that's on him."

"When we free the captain, I'm sailing away from this place and never looking back."

"You better take us with you." Hale sighed, scraping the last bit of soup from his bowl and popping the bread in his mouth.

Much to his surprise, Griff tilted on her stool, resting her head wearily against the meat of his bicep. "You help me get him free and we'll take you wherever you want to go."

Hale looked down at her, spiky red hair sticking out in wild angles. An emotion blossomed in his chest, strange and unfamiliar. It wasn't lust, that he was well versed in. And it wasn't love, or at least not the heartache he had briefly experienced when a new blossom came into his life ripe for the picking. This was…different. He felt fond of Griff. Protective. Grateful for her presence. Grateful that he wasn't alone. What was that? He shrugged, and moved to wrap his arm around her narrow shoulders. He rested his head on the top of hers. "It's a deal," he said softly. He paused but couldn't help himself. "Augustina."

She punched him in the stomach.

CHAPTER 14

Hale had a new favorite thing. A bath. He had flashed his best smile to each and every serving woman who had carried buckets of hot water upstairs to fill the copper tub. And when he stepped in—heaven. He had, honest to gods, died and been taken up to the Sower's golden fields. He had bathed nearly every day of his life but never—*never* had he appreciated the magic of the warm water like he did today. It relaxed muscles he didn't know he had, washed off the dirt and the salt and the blood. Cal's blood.

Hale's elation dimmed as weariness swept through him. Cal should have been with him here, second-guessing Hale's harebrained scheme at first, then throwing himself into his role with surprising gusto. It wasn't right that he wasn't here. This world wasn't right without Cal. How he would face his mother? She had seen Cal wounded on the ground...but she didn't know. Not for sure. Surely, she must have held out hope. How could he look her in the eye and tell her he'd failed? That he couldn't save him?

Hale wallowed in these dark thoughts until the water grew murky and tepid. Finally, he pulled his tanned body from the bath, wrapping a fluffy towel around himself. He shaved the scratchy beginning of a beard and was combing his hair when a knock came on the door. He opened it to a pretty, blonde serving girl holding a package in her hands. "Your clothes, sir," she said, taking in Hale's bare chest with wide eyes and cheeks turning scarlet.

Hale opened the door wider and leaned against it, holding his towel around his waist. "Theo must have the prettiest serving girls in all of Sryalta," Hale said, his deep voice purring.

The serving girl turned even redder, her eyes flicking from the ground to Hale's chest and back again. That bath had him feeling like his old self. But he wasn't here for pleasure, so he took the package from her outstretched hands and thanked her before closing the door with a twinge of regret. Now was not a time to get distracted.

Hale unwrapped the package of clothes, bracing himself for the shock of Theo's terrible fashion sense. The innkeeper dressed like a logger; Hale didn't imagine the man knew much about a fine suit. Yet he was pleasantly surprised by what he unearthed beneath the twine and brown paper. A chocolate-brown velvet jacket, a purple waistcoat flecked with gold houndstooth, and a pair of fine tan trousers with a sheen of gold, if you tilted them a certain way. A crisp white shirt, purple tie, clean underclothes, a gold pocket watch, and—the shoes. Hale held them up to admire them. These were good. The brown and caramel leather brogues would match the rest of the suit perfectly. "Not bad, Theo. Not bad."

When he had tied his shoe laces and tucked in the gold pocket watch, he faced himself in the mirror and felt a most peculiar sense of relief. The past few days had been picking him apart, piece by piece, and finally, in this suit, he felt gathered back together. Almost whole.

A knock sounded on the door, followed by Griff's muffled voice. "You take longer than a girl to get ready."

Hale pulled the door open with a grin. "One doesn't rush perfection."

His next witty comment died on his tongue as the sight of Griff temporarily added his brain. Hale hardly recognized her. Theo had found her a red wig and soft, copper curls cascaded over one bare shoulder. Her dress was deep purple trimmed in gold, matching Hale's waistcoat, but it was a masterpiece of tailoring, dipping low to display a creamy bosom, cinching tight around Griff's tiny waist, flaring out into a draped skirt embroidered with intricate geometric designs. As Hale's examination returned upward, he saw that Griff's face was expertly painted—dark kohl and mascara making her green eyes seem twice as big, stain on her lips making them seem twice as kissable. A pair of glittering gold earrings hung from her ears, shadowing the delicate curve of her long neck.

"You were saying about perfection?" She smirked.

"Now I know why Theo was so enamored," Hale said.

"You don't look half bad yourself," she said, swallowing. Hale knew he did cut an impressive figure.

"Where were you hiding those all this time?" he asked, pointing to her half-exposed bosom. "Seriously, I feel like I should have noticed."

Griff smacked Hale's arm with her fan. "Don't get too attached. This is a one-time only thing. For the captain."

Hale offered his arm, and Griff took it, walking into the hallway. "Beauties like that deserve to be free, not buried under some sad, old smock."

Griff smacked him again with her fan, this time in the chest.

"I don't think that's what that fan is for."

"It's exactly what it's for," she muttered.

Sim Rakoni's auction house—called the Forum—was an impressive establishment. It sprawled across two city blocks, soaring several stories—the most solid-looking building Hale had seen in Sryalta. Two burly guards at the entrance patted them down for weapons before letting them pass. Hale hadn't brought a weapon. The only way out of this place was with Sim Rakoni's begrudging blessing, and his mother at his side.

Hale thought he knew the type of man the slaver was. He had encountered them before, amongst the Se Caelus's political elite. Proud, ruthless. They had their own twisted sense of honor, but they stood by it. If Hale challenged Rakoni in public, the man wouldn't be able to back down. And if Hale won fair and square, Rakoni would abide by it, as much as he might hate it. That was the only way he could ensure anyone would continue dealing with him. To be a man of his word.

Once inside, Hale and Griff were met by a voluptuous waitress who handed them each glasses of sparkling wine. Hale surveyed the interior of the building with interest. The Forum could rival any gambling hall in Se Caelus. The hall had a soaring, arched ceiling decorated by frescoes of intertwined bodies. Elaborate carvings and gold leaf adorned the tall columns, broad balconies, and many tables spread before them. At the far end, a stage stood empty, no doubt where the slave auctions were held. Hale fought to hold his scowl at bay.

"Okay," Griff said under her breath. "What's the plan?"

"Head to the hazard tables. Go on such a winning streak that Sim Rakoni can't help but take notice."

"Is that all?"

"Leave this to me," Hale said with a toothy grin. He had found his table. Across the room. Pudgy dealer in a too-tight suit, another stickman stifling a yawn. Well, it was these fellows' lucky day. Things were about to get interesting.

"You know how to play?" he whispered to Griff as they approached the empty table.

"We played on the ship. I'm no good, though. Don't play often enough to remember what nicks what."

Hale chuckled softly, laying an Aprican gold crown on the table. "That's kind of an important part."

"I said I was no good, didn't I?" She took a sip of wine and flashed a simpering smile to the dealer.

"Sir. My lady," the dealer said, setting down a small stack of red chips. The stick man passed Hale a pair of green dice. Hale picked them up, letting out a slow breath. This was it. He threw.

Hazard was a complex game, and the speed at which it was played made it all the more opaque. Roll the dice once to establish your main, or the number you'd be rolling based on. Your main determined what numbers threw in, or nicked, your main. Throwing aces or deuce-ace was a loss. Any other roll was your chance. If this happened, keep rolling until you roll your chance, in which case you won, or you rolled your main, in which case you lost. Somehow it made sense to him. Other players could bet on the shooter—wagering on whether he'd win or lose. Hale didn't like to play that way, though. Hale liked to be right in the action. The shooter. Because Hale had uncanny luck with the dice. They were his friends, his sage companions. They hadn't let him down yet.

Griff drummed her fingers on the side of the table, betraying her nervousness, as he began to play.

Bet, roll, nick.

Bet, roll, chance.

Hit the chance.

Methodically, Hale began to play, getting into the rhythm, ignoring the rapidly-growing stack of chips on the table. He felt the moment when Griff's nerves switched to excitement. She began jumping and clapping with every roll, leaning over the table to check the dice as they landed. He didn't blame her. He probably would have thought himself crazy too, claiming to be able to win back their family with a pair of dice. But for whatever reason, this was his gift. He was preternaturally lucky. And he'd be damned if he wasn't going to milk it for all it was worth.

A crowd had grown around the table now, other patrons drawn by Griff's cheering and the dealers' disbelieving exclamations. They were betting on his streak, winning when he won.

Hale's pile had grown almost substantial enough to draw the attention of the owners. It was time to draw some real attention.

The stickman pushed the dice Hale's way with a breath of anticipation. The man wasn't yawning now.

"All in," Hale said. "Pass." He was betting that he'd win. Betting it all.

Gasps went up around the table, and Griff grabbed his arm. "Hale, are you mad?"

He looked down at her with a wink. She was playing her role perfectly, though perhaps she wasn't truly playing at anything anymore. "Nothing ventured, nothing gained."

The dealer looked at him with a nod, his jowls quivering.

Hale shook, and the dice chattered like teeth inside his hand. He released and they rolled, bouncing off the back wall of the table.

"Eight," the dealer called out.

With a main of eight, he needed to roll eight or twelve to win. It was almost too easy.

He took the dice back, looking at Griff, whose hands were clutched in front of her mouth, her eyes wide with tension.

"Wish me luck, darling," he said with a grin before rolling. He didn't need to look.

The crowd around the table exploded into cheers and cries of disbelief, one man even jumping up and down.

"Twelve!" the dealer called as Griff leaped into his arms, hugging him tightly as he spun her around. "By the Sower, Hale, you're going to kill me before we're done!"

The cheering was dying down, and the dealer was counting out Hale's winnings. His chips had changed to black, but his stacks still took up much of the table.

A hush fell over the table, and Hale turned, his arm still around Griff's waist. *Yes.* This was what he had been hoping for. Counting on. There was a man striding across the floor, trailed by two uniformed guards with swords at their hips.

"Let me guess," Hale said. "Our very own Sim Rakoni."

"In the flesh," Griff breathed.

CHAPTER 15

Sim Rakoni was not what Hale had expected. For one, he was old—his hair was snow-white, crisply cut at chin length. But when he reached the table, Hale saw that the man was not frail, far from it. His skin was tanned, his handsome features framed by a neat, white goatee. He wore a light gray suit over a waistcoat of sky blue, which matched the icy color of his eyes. He had a vibrancy—an intensity that Hale had only seen before in some of Se Caelus's most charismatic politicians. This was not a man to trifle with.

"It's been many years since I've had such a streak of luck at the Forum. I had to congratulate the man himself," Rakoni said. His voice was smooth like velvet, his words honeyed.

"It's an honor to meet you, sir," Hale replied, figuring that sucking up was the best way to go. "It's a fine place you have here."

"What brings you to Sryalta...?" Rakoni quirked a white eyebrow, asking for Hale's name.

"Hale Firena. And this lovely lady is my companion, Augustina."

Griff flashed a sweet smile and dipped a curtsy while Rakoni nodded his head, watching Hale out of the corner of his eye. Hale's name meant something to him. He had hidden it well, but there was a tiny sliver of recognition. He definitely had Hale's mother.

"And I came to Sryalta to make a wager. With you," Hale said.

The crowd gasped slightly at Hale's impertinence, whispers blossoming like flowers after the rain.

Rakoni smiled, a tight-lipped gesture that didn't melt the ice in his eyes. "What kind of wager?"

"You have two prisoners that I would like the opportunity of winning. An Aprican noblewoman. Brea Firena. And a sailor, Captain Brimmer." He wanted to ask for Emery and her mother too, but he didn't dare. If his information was correct, those two didn't have a price on their head. He couldn't have Rakoni offering to give him Emery and her mother when what Hale really couldn't leave here without was Brimmer and *his* mother. He needed to be clear in his offer, start from a position of strength. Her offered a silent apology. Perhaps he could find some way to buy their freedom when this was all done.

"I know of whom you speak. But I don't gamble away my prisoners. Especially not two who have garnered such…interest."

"What's the matter? Afraid you can't beat me?" Hale stepped forward, puffing his chest up.

Rakoni's eyes narrowed. The entire stretch of the Forum was silent. The music had stopped, dealers had stopped shuffling. From the far corners to the top balcony, everyone was watching Rakoni and the tall, handsome hazard player who had the gall to challenge him.

Griff clutched his arm, her nails biting through the thick velvet of his jacket.

Rakoni stepped forward until he was shoulder-to-shoulder with Hale, his lips close to Hale's ear. But before he could say whatever whispered threat he intended, Hale plunged ahead. "I meant no disrespect," he whispered. "But I needed to get your attention. It is the role of the young upstart to challenge the venerated master, is it not?"

Rakoni stiffened, cocking his head to examine Hale.

"One wager," Hale continued. "You win, you've increased your wealth and your reputation only grows larger. I win, I take two troublesome slaves off your hands, and you never see me again. I spread word far and wide that your ruthlessness is only outmatched by the hospitality of the Forum."

The man let out a little breath of laughter, shaking his head. He stepped back. "What did you say your name was?"

"Hale Firena, sir." Hale offered his hand.

Sim Rakoni took his hand, shaking it slowly. He spoke loudly, so the gathered crowd could hear. "You, Hale Firena, are the cockiest bastard who ever walked into the Forum. Reminds me of myself at your age. You will have your wager." He flashed a bright white, toothy grin and the those who had been waiting with bated breath broke into applause and cheers. "Karl, bring us a bottle of my finest scotch," Rakoni said to one of the bodyguards. "Dealer, tally up Mr. Firena's winnings."

Hale felt an enormous coil of tension unwind through his spine, and the blood began flowing back into his arm as Griff released her death grip.

Rakoni ushered them to a nearby table, where he perched on a leather high-back stool, pulling a rolled cigarette from his pocket. He offered one to Hale, who declined, taking a seat across the table. Griff sat on the chair next to him, clutching the edge of the table to steady her shaking hands.

"Quite a streak of luck you had." Rakoni blew out a puff of smoke. "It's been a while since I've seen such a run. Would have figured you were cheating, if you weren't using my own dice."

"I wouldn't dream of cheating you, sir," Hale said, trying to don a mask of the eager ingénue.

"Yet you dream of coming into my club and forcing a wager down my throat?"

"That's an unfortunate necessity. You see, bandits...*borrowed* two members of our party. We're here to get them back."

"What's your offer?"

Hale took a breath. "One round of hazard. I win, we take our two friends. You win, you keep my winnings."

"You offer me my own money back? You'll have to do better than that."

Hale held up a hand. "My winnings, and the two of us."

"Hale!" Griff hissed, her face turning pale. Her fingernails were now clenching painfully into his thigh under the table.

Rakoni looked between them thoughtfully before leaning across the table and twisting a lock of Griff's hair around his index finger. She sat as still as a statue as Rakoni examined her with obvious interest, digging her fingers tighter into Hale's flesh. Finally, Rakoni withdrew his hand and the curl bounced back. Griff released her grip with a tense exhale of breath. Damn, the girl was strong!

"I can see the charms presented by your young companion, but what do you propose I do with you?"

"Pleasure slave?" Hale shrugged with a sympathetic grin. "I'm sure I could entertain some of Sryalta's lonely widows."

To Hale's surprise, Rakoni burst out laughing. "By the Sower, boy, you do have a pair on you. All right. The two of you for the two of them. One round of hazard. But I throw the dice. You bet."

Hale's mind raced. His luck should still hold if he was betting, but he couldn't predict what Rakoni might try to do to tilt the odds against Hale. How could he pull this out of the fire? "I'd prefer to throw," Hale said, stalling while he raced for a solution to even the playing field.

"I'm sure you would." Rakoni chuckled. "But that's my wager. Take it or leave it."

Brilliance struck Hale like lightning. "On one condition. I place my wager silently with the dealer. You don't know whether I'm betting on you to pass or not pass."

Mirth glimmered in the man's blue eyes. "Very well. A fair addition to the terms. You have your bet."

Hale grinned and stood, throwing back the glass of whisky that had been set before him. "Let's go."

Rakoni stood and strolled back to the hazard table. The crowd parted for him like waves breaking on the rocks.

"I hope you know what you're doing," Griff whispered in his ear. "You had no right to wager with my freedom."

"You said yourself you were going to trade yourself for the captain. I'm sorry, but it was necessary. This whole nightmare is almost over."

"Can you win?" she asked, her voice laced with desperation—and something else. Something he had never heard from Griff. Fear. She would rather than die than be a slave again. He could see it in her eyes as he turned to her. "Trust me," he said, leaning down to kiss her on her cheek.

Sim Rakoni was handing his jacket to one of his bodyguards and rolling up the starched sleeves of his shirt. A man like Rakoni would want to win. Would be good at winning. So Hale should bet on him to pass. Unless…a frown crept onto his face. Unless the man knew Hale would expect him to try to win, so he'd try to lose instead. Not that the man could control the dice…but a seasoned player…could make a difference.

"Why so serious, Mr. Firena?" Rakoni turned with a predatory smile. "Not having fun anymore?"

Hale straightened and smiled. "To the contrary, sir. Life is lived on the edge of wager."

"Isn't that the truth? Give Mr. Firena a piece of paper and a pen. He'll be writing down his bet."

The dealer passed him a thick piece of paper and a fine pen. Hale bent over to write and found himself hesitating. Pass or no pass? Normally, his instincts fired crystal clear. He knew what to do, which horse, which number, which card. In his easy arrogance was a truth, a kernel of intuition that had never steered him wrong. But something about Rakoni's slick smile, Griff's desperate plea. Cal. This place, these clothes. Dirt and blood and loss. They had thrown him. He wasn't the same Hale that he had been before—carefree and cocky. People depended on him now. His mother, Griff. It was all fine to wager and bluster. But when it mattered, was it enough? Was he enough?

Pass or no pass? It should have been simple. The most obvious thing in the world. Heads or tails. Pass or no pass.

"We're waiting, Mr. Firena," Sim Rakoni said.

Hale closed his eyes, trying to center himself, but found only tumult. Now was not the time for his luck to desert him. Now was not the time to overthink. He needed to go back to the basics. The core essence. And what was the most fundamental rule of gambling? *The house always wins.* He would bet that Rakoni would win.

Pass, Hale wrote, folding the paper once and handing it to the dealer.

Griff's eyes were wild with panic now. She had seen the hesitation, the shaking of Hale's hand on the pen. She knew that he doubted. *It'll be okay,* he wanted to assure her. *It'll be okay,* he wanted to assure himself.

The stickman pushed the green dice across the table to Sim Rakoni. With casual grace, the man picked up the dice and rolled them. They clicked to the end of the table, where they came to rest. Nine was his main. Damnation. Where some of the other mains had two rolls that could nick them, there was only one roll that could nick a nine—another nine.

Hale straightened and met Sim Rakoni's eyes with a bold smile. "An excellent roll," he said.

Rakoni took the dice again, to a collective inhale of breath. The tension in the room was palpable. Only Hale knew whether he wanted Rakoni to win or lose; not even Griff knew what number she should be rooting for. He took the dice again and with painful slowness, shook them in his fist. His eyes never left Hale's as he threw.

Click-click, click-click.

They landed with the weight of a thousand prayers. "Nicks!" the dealer called incredulously. The crowd cheered for Sim Rakoni—for his expert roll.

Griff pressed herself to Hale's side. "Tell me you wrote pass on that little piece of paper." Her knuckles were white.

The dealer unfolded the paper and read from it. "PASS!" he shouted, holding it aloft. "The young man wins!"

Griff collapsed against him, her forehead resting on his arm. "Thank the Sower. You lucky bastard."

Rakoni's smile of congratulation was tight-lipped. "Well played, Mr. Firena. Do you care to make one more wager?"

Griff's nails of doom were back, biting into his bicep.

"What do you propose?" Hale asked.

"One more roll. Same terms if I win."

"And if I win?" Hale looked down at Griff.

"No," she hissed. "Do not."

"There were two other women who were captured with us," said Hale. "The wife and daughter of Sim Chiron. Free them. And grant us all safe passage from this place. Get us to Maradis, the capital of Alesia. In style," he amended.

Rakoni snorted. "Is that all?"

"Those are my terms."

"Hale, you wool-headed fool," Griff whispered. "He has you now."

A cautious man would have taken his mother and Captain Brimmer and run for the hills. But Hale was not a cautious man. And he had realized there was nothing keeping Rakoni from slitting all their throats when they were out of sight. There was honor among thieves, but he didn't know how far it extended. Plus, it had never sat well with him to leave Emery and her mother behind. A place like this would eat up an innocent girl like that.

"We have another wager," Rakoni said, seizing the dice once again. "Get him another piece of paper."

Hale found himself pondering again. If he was Rakoni, he'd try to lose now, to throw Hale off. But he must have known that Hale would guess that. Or maybe he would guess that Hale would guess, so he'd plan for a winning roll, expecting Hale to expect him to throw the match.

His choice was easier this time. His intuition, his luck, flowed through him more freely. He had come back to himself. Rakoni was a man who had to be seen winning. That was why he had offered this second bet. He would expect Hale to think he would try a new strategy. But for a man like Rakoni, there was only one strategy: Win.

Pass, he wrote on the paper.

He nodded solemnly to Rakoni, who had lost his smile. With intense focus, he threw the dice. "Six!" the dealer called.

Hale wrapped an arm around Griff as Rakoni threw again. But he already knew what it would be. The tingle inside told him—his luck would hold.

EPILOGUE

"Your expertise is quite impressive, Sa Firena. Word of your fine vintages has traveled even this far." Hale and his mother sat in two plush velvet chairs opposite Guildmaster Alban, the head of Alesia's Vintner's Guild. Brea had put in an application to join.

"When you love what you do, it doesn't feel like work," Brea said graciously. "I'm eager to get back to it."

"I must admit, I'll be pleased to have you within our guild rather than as a competitor to it."

Hale sat politely, half-listening to them discuss the location of Brea's new winery. There was an old warehouse in the north of the Port Quarter that was well located and going for a good price. Brea wouldn't be able to grow her grapes here—no one could, what with western Alesia's cool, wet climate—but she could source her grapes from across the Cascadian mountains and brew and bottle here.

Brea looked as beautiful and full of color as she once had, in a bronze dress that highlighted the gold of her hair. Rakoni had kept his word and had gotten them passage to Alesia on a finely-appointed vessel. The voyage from Sryalta had healed some wounds, though other, deeper cuts would take more time. *Like Cal,* Hale thought with a pang. Sometimes he and his mother sat in silence thinking of him, while other nights they told stories, shared memories. At least they had each other. That was enough for now—to get them through.

He had said goodbye to Griff yesterday out on the docks. He had given her a share of his winnings from the hazard game, and she and Brimmer had bought a little ship. Not as grand as the Nightingale, but the captain assured him that they would steal a grander one soon enough. Though Hale was sad to see her go, he was glad she was flying free once again. She had let Theo down as easily as she could after returning the money they had borrowed, explaining that she just couldn't see herself married and settled down.

"Stop and see me whenever you're in Maradis?" Hale had asked. "I'll want all the stories of your grand adventures."

"Somehow, I think you'll manage to have a grand adventure or two of your own right here. Maradis won't know what hit it." Griff had grinned. She'd been back in trousers and a jacket, a broad-brimmed hat pulled over her fiery hair. Though she had been beautiful in the dress, this suited her beauty more. He saw that now.

He'd watched them raise their sails, stark against the blustery gray sky. He'd stood there until they'd been past the breakwater and out of sight. Maradis felt a little more alien without Griff in it. But Hale had turned, shrugging it off. Griff had said so herself—here was a whole new city, ripe for the picking. There was fun to be had. Women to be courted. Trouble to be found.

"Hale?" Brea's hand was on Hale's arm. She was standing. He started, looking from her to the guildmaster. They were done here. Hale stood. "Apologies," he said.

The guildmaster walked them through the dark-paneled hallways of the Vintner's guildhall, out onto the front steps. They stood on Guilder's Row, an impressive stretch of buildings housing each of the ten guilds. The sky in the background was gray, sputtering rain. Maradis was a city painted in shades of gray, Hale had quickly realized. He would miss the blue skies of his home.

The guildmaster shook his mother's hand, then Hale's. "What about you, son? Will you be joining the guild as well? You're past the age to start as an apprentice, but we could get you brought up to speed quickly enough, if you have your mother's talents."

Brea looked at Hale. "I'm afraid Hale may be taking Maradis's business world by storm. He's supernaturally lucky. I keep telling him he should go into finance. Stocks."

The guildmaster raised an eyebrow appraisingly. "You know, you might consider exploring the Confectioner's Guild." He pointed to a white marble building a few down the row. "One of the most influential and venerated guilds. Plus, I know the guildmaster, Kasper, myself."

"Chocolates?" Brea asked with amusement. "I'm not sure that would be up Hale's alley."

"You'd be surprised, Sa Firena. The culinary arts call with a siren song. I have a feeling a lucky fellow like Hale would be well suited for confections."

Hale considered. He had enjoyed rolling those caramels with Emery. But that was a thin slice of experience to base his career on. Why did this man seem so certain it would be a fit?

As he looked down the stone street, he caught sight of a vision that stilled his breath. A woman—unlike any he had ever seen. Dark hair so black, it looked blue whipping in the wind. Olive skin, dark, arching eyebrows and full lips that were ripe for kissing. A burgundy dress hugged her generous curves, rippling against her legs in the wind. She wore a necklace of colorful beads at her swan-like throat. She was, without a doubt, the most beautiful woman he had ever seen.

Guildmaster Alban followed his gaze and let out a chuckle. "Master Sable. She's one of the Confectioner's Guild's most promising young members."

Sable. Hale wanted to roll the word on his tongue like a fine bourbon. He turned to Alban, straightening his waistcoat. "You know, I think the Confectioner's Guild might be the place for me after all. Can you make an introduction?"

THE END

FROM THE AUTHOR

Thank you so much for taking the time to read *The Confectioner's Exile!* I hope you've enjoyed reading about Hale's adventures as much as I enjoyed writing them!

Reader reviews are incredibly important to indie authors like me, and so it would mean the world to me if you took a few minutes to leave an honest review wherever you buy books online. It doesn't have to be much; a few words can make the difference in helping a future reader give the book a chance.

If you're interested in receiving updates, giveaways, and advanced copies of upcoming books, sign up for my mailing list at http://claireluana.com! As a thank you for signing up, you will receive a free ebook!

And don't miss *The Confectioner's Guild,* Book One in the Confectioner Chronicles!

Read on for a Sneak Peek.

THE CONFECTIONER'S GUILD

CLAIRE LUANA

CHAPTER 1

Wren had learned early on that trouble comes in all sorts of packages. Even vanilla ones with rose petal frosting.

"Tell me about these cupcakes," a cold voice demanded from the storefront.

Wren froze on her stool, her ears perked to listen, the cocoa bean she held in her hand forgotten.

"What would you like to know?" asked Master Oldrick, his tone light but wary.

"Everything."

Wren set down her husking knife on the worktable with the rest of the cracked beans, wiping her hands on her streaked apron. She wanted a look at this customer. She crept across the worn tiles of the kitchen and slowly slid open one of the doors leading to the display case in the front room of Master Oldrick's confectionery shop. A wave of cold air hit her, the ice that lined the case chilling her face as well as the chocolates. It was a blessed respite from the stickiness of the kitchen, where the air hung limp in August's hot breath.

Master Oldrick was babbling about the cupcakes now, clearly unsure of the nature of the man's interest. "True, cupcakes are the territory of the Baker's Guild, but I've some friends in that guild, and they don't mind us having a little fun with the cupcakes. It's the frosting that sets ours apart. Pure confectional art. The frosting on this one's so like a rose that you can practically smell its perfume. The ladies love them—they fly off the shelves."

The customer was a stranger, but the cupcake in his hand was not. It was one of Wren's. Only she could pipe the frosting just right, each petal like a rosy-hued sunset. Master Oldrick's arthritis was far too bad for him to perform such delicate work, and the other apprentices, Tate and Hazel, were all right for rolling truffle balls and stirring caramel, but they lacked her steady hand with a piping bag, despite being a few months younger than her sixteen years. Each of those cupcakes had taken her ten minutes to decorate, ten minutes scrunched over the countertop as beads of sweat dribbled down her knees and elbows.

Master Oldrick was continuing his detailed exposition of the cupcakes' finer features, discussing the third-generation ownership of the mill they purchased flour from, the fine sugar imported from Aprica, the fresh cream skimmed off the milk of dairy cows who enjoyed only the finest pastureland below the foothills of Mount Luminis.

The customer held up a hand and Master Oldrick fell silent. Wren narrowed her eyes. Who was this man, and what was his interest in the cupcakes?

"Who made the cupcakes?" the man demanded.

"Ahh," Master Oldrick said nervously. "My apprentice Wren," he said, rubbing his neck with a gnarled hand. His gaze flicked to the far display case, where Wren peeked out between the rows of caramels and chocolate chews.

The man turned and his eyes, steely blue above the high collar of his navy coat, met hers. "I'll speak with this Wren."

"I'll fetch her," Master Oldrick said with a bob of his head.

Wren stood and slammed the door shut, her mind whirring. Despite the oppressive heat of the late afternoon, her body had gone cold.

Master Oldrick's hands were shaking as he came into the kitchen.

"What does he want?" she hissed. "Who is he?"

"I don't know," Master Oldrick said. "But he has a stern way about him. Was there something wrong with the cupcakes? Could the ingredients have spoiled?"

"No!" she said, affronted. Master Oldrick knew the quality of her work was her only currency in this world. "I would never let such a thing happen."

"I know." He sighed. "You're the best apprentice I've ever had, woman or no."

She rolled her eyes. It wasn't the first time she'd heard such antiquated views from Oldrick. She found it best to ignore them.

"I'll stand by your work," he continued. "Now don't keep the man waiting."

Wren straightened her stained apron and attempted to smooth the frizzy auburn halo that wreathed her head in this humidity. She marched into the front of the shop, back straight, head high.

"You asked for me, sir?" she said, getting her first proper look at the customer. He was a tall, thin man with a horsey face topped with thick, dark brows that threatened to join as one. He had an impressive shock of black hair brushed to one side in a fashion that managed to look both windswept and carefully manicured. His slender fingers held her exquisite cupcake before her, as if he were offering her a rose.

His examination of her was as obvious as her scrutiny of him no doubt had been. What did he see? Milky pale skin, elfin features, a small mouth puckered in nervousness? From the slight sneer of his lip, it appeared he found her wanting.

"Did you make this cupcake?" That cold voice again.

She shivered involuntarily. "Yes. Why?"

He ignored her question. "I need you to come with me."

"What? Where?" Wren took a step back.

He put the cupcake back in its tasteful pink-and-white-striped box before deftly retying the white ribbon in a perfect bow. And then, task complete, he came around the counter in two strides, grasping her elbow.

"Master Oldrick!" Wren cried. She struggled against his iron grip, panic rising through her like a pot left to boil.

Master Oldrick bustled through the swinging doors. "What's this? No customers behind the counter."

"He's trying to take me somewhere," Wren explained, trying to draw her master's attention to the more pressing issue at hand.

"Now, sir, what's this all about?" asked Oldrick.

"Guild business," the man said.

"I'm her master; she's got no business with the Guild that doesn't concern me. Is she in some kind of trouble?" Master Oldrick asked. "I'm sure whatever it is, we can come to terms."

The man readjusted his fingers on Wren's arm, tightening his clammy grip. With his other hand, he pulled a card from his pocket. "I am Grandmaster Callidus of the Confectioner's Guild. I set the terms. And this girl is coming with me."

Wren glowered at the grandmaster from across the jostling coach, trying to keep the embers of fear tamped down with the weight of her anger. It was a losing battle. She rubbed her damp palms on her dress, curling her fingers into the thin fabric to still her shaking hands. Whatever was going on, it couldn't be good.

"Where are we going?" she asked for the third time.

For the third time, he looked at her with contemptuous flick of his gaze before his icy stare returned to the window.

Despite her unanswered questions, Wren had been keeping a close eye past the lace curtains of the carriage and had a strong suspicion of their destination. As they turned off the packed dirt road onto the smooth granite stones of the Maradis town's center, her prediction was confirmed: The Confectioner's Guildhall. Just visible in the distance, nine guildhalls sat like petulant children at the knee of their mother, the gray behemoth Tradehouse where the guilds did business with each other and the rest of the city. The Confectioner's Guildhall was a massive marble monolith resting in the place of honor at the Tradehouse's right hand and was arguably the most magnificent structure of the impressive specimens that lined Guilder's Row.

The carriage came to a stop in front of the steps of the Guildhall and the coachman opened the door. Callidus swept out before her and quickly resumed his position as her captor, grasping her arm as soon as she cleared the steps. It was clear he didn't intend to let her escape. Wren's stomach flipped. What was there to escape from?

Wren struggled up the towering steps of the Guildhall, scraping her shins as Callidus pulled her up. Five steps for the five levels of the Guild: apprentice, journeyman, artisan, master, and grandmaster. Some designer had been so intent on his symbolism that he had thrown practicality straight out the window.

As servants in the Guild's brown and gold livery opened the wide wooden doors before them, Wren found herself pulled through the antechamber of the Guildhall for the second time in her life. And for the second time, she found herself wishing she had something better to wear.

Her first glimpse of the Guildhall had been four years ago. That time, it had been Master Oldrick's fat fingers gripping the flesh of her arm. She'd been a grimy orphan, fresh off the streets of Maradis.

It had started innocently enough. She had been rifling through the trash in the alley behind his shop and had found a worn piping bag, mostly empty save for a dollop of shimmering green frosting. Any other street kid would have squirted the whole bag of sugar into their mouth, but the frosting had called to her. She knew such an act would be a waste, a sacrilege. Crouched under the eaves of the building to keep warm, she had grasped the smooth parchment paper of the bag and decorated the hard shell of the snowbank with a pattern of ivy leaves. The leaves had sparkled against the snow in the low light of the alley, mesmerizing her, pulling her into a daydream where she was surrounded by lush green foliage rather than frozen garbage.

Master Oldrick had woken her with a kick in the dim gray morning, but as she'd scrambled away down the alley, he'd called to her. "Stop!"

She'd kept running.

"I'll feed you!" he'd called.

She had frozen, looking over one shoulder, her gnawing stomach compelling her to turn around. He had fed her half a loaf of warm bread smeared with butter and jam, along with a glass of sweet milk. Once she had eaten, he'd made her scrub her hands in scalding water until they'd turned pink and had given her an audition. Wren had swirled ganache, puffed powdered sugar, drizzled white chocolate and piped more frosting. When she had tried to sneak a taste of the ganache, Master Oldrick had whacked her hand so hard with a wooden spoon that she'd felt the vibrations in her teeth.

"Never. Ever. Eat. The. Confections," he'd said.

But despite her faux pas, she had passed his test. Because that afternoon, he had marched her, dressed in a tattered woolen smock, into the marble cavern of the Confectioner's Guildhall. And she had become his apprentice.

The interior of the Guildhall looked exactly the same as it had four years ago, but for the exchange of one sour-faced captor for another. The walls were made of creamy veined marble, and the tall pillars around the circular antechamber rose to form a massive dome coated in gold filigree. A magnificent crystal chandelier hung from the dome, dusting the room with sparkles of sugary light.

Wren eyed Callidus sideways as she struggled to match his pace. Guildmembers seemed to part before him as he walked, nodding deferentially and sidestepping out of his way. He didn't acknowledge any of them with so much as a smile or nod in return. So he *was* someone important. And, Wren decided, he was most definitely an ass.

They ascended a twisting staircase at the far end of the antechamber, heading towards the upper floors. Where were they going? She could ask Callidus, but she didn't want to give him the satisfaction of knowing that his silent treatment was flustering her. He probably wouldn't tell her, anyway.

They continued up two more levels until they reached a floor that was hushed and empty. Two guards in brown and gold flanked the top of the stair, their golden spears resting on the polished parquet floor. Their uniforms bore the Guild's symbol on the breast, a golden whisk and spoon crossed like the letter "X."

Wren's heart hammered in her chest as they came to a halt before a carved mahogany door. Why had she been summoned here? Was she being kicked out of the Guild? Had there been something wrong with the cupcakes? They were so deep in the Guildhall, if she screamed now, would anyone hear her?

Callidus released her arm and rapped on the door three times with his pale knuckles.

CHAPTER 2

The door swung open and Wren almost laughed in relief at the sight. A short ruddy man with a rotund belly and a thick head of snowy white hair stood before her. He reminded her of nothing so much as one of her cupcakes, the red velvet kind sprinkled with coconut shavings.

"Come in, come in," he said, waving them into the room enthusiastically. He wore a crisp shirt with the sleeves rolled up, revealing substantial forearms covered with downy white hair. As she passed him, she caught a whiff of butterscotch.

"Have a seat, my dear. Have a seat," he repeated, motioning to one of the two studded leather chairs that sat before his huge desk. Not at all the dungeon she had expected—the room was bright and cheerful, with tall windows letting in streams of sluggish summer sun.

Wren sat, smoothing her faded cotton dress over her knees.

"Callidus, feel free to sit," the man said, motioning to the other chair.

She shied away from it involuntarily.

"I'll stand," Callidus replied, leaning against a bookshelf by the door.

"Of course you will." The man paused for a moment. "I hope Callidus didn't scare you too terribly. He lacks something of a bedside manner."

Wren laughed, a forced bark that belied her nervousness. "He was… mysterious," she admitted, thinking it best not to antagonize him.

"Well, let's put the mystery to an end. I am Guildmaster Kasper, Head of the Confectioner's Guild. And you are?"

"Wren," she said. "Wren Confectioner," she added, in the Alesian style. In the country of Alesia, a guildmember who didn't wish to keep their father's surname, or who didn't know their father's name, could take the name of their craft as their surname.

"It's a delight to meet you, Wren," Kasper said. "Did Callidus explain why we summoned you?"

"No."

"Of course not." He pursed his lips. "You're no doubt wondering why you're here. Callidus, where are those cupcakes?"

Callidus dropped the box on the desk between them before resuming his statue-like pose against the bookcase.

"Excellent," Kasper said, opening the box. He removed one of the cupcakes and turned it before him, admiring it from various angles. "These are magnificent, my dear. I've known masters who couldn't make such masterpieces. You're what, an artisan?"

"Apprentice, guildmaster."

"Apprentice!" his brown eyes flew open. "For how long?"

"Four years, guildmaster."

"Four years!" He harrumphed. "Outrageous. You could cook circles around some of my best guildmembers. Your master will be hearing from me."

"Thank you, guildmaster," she said, keeping the vindicated smile from her face. She knew Master Oldrick had been lying about her not being ready for a promotion within the Guild, she just hadn't figured out what to do about it. Oldrick wasn't a bad man—only greedy. And promoting her meant paying her higher wages.

"I can tell you have a gift for confections. Such gifts are rare, even within the Guild," Kasper said. His eyes gleamed in the sunlight as he studied her, setting the cupcake before her. "You've sampled your confections, haven't you?"

She shook her head. "Master Oldrick forbids it." More for the customers. And the cash register.

Guildmaster Kasper sputtered, slapping his hand on the desk. "This Oldrick fellow, I like him less and less! How do you make chocolate if you don't taste it?"

"I follow the recipe. And get it right the first time." No need to mention that she had stolen a taste or two when Oldrick wasn't looking.

"Quite right, quite right. I suppose that explains how skinny you are. No respectable confectioner should be skinny!" He slapped the girth of his stomach and laughed, a warm husky sound. "Confections are what make the world go 'round, don't you agree?"

Wren cracked a smile despite herself. His enthusiasm was infectious. "The world would be a happier place if that were true."

"But it *is* true," he said, as if he had a secret he couldn't wait to share. Kasper reached in the breast pocket of his shirt and pulled out a heavy gold coin. It was an Alesian gold crown, more money than Wren made in a year. He handed it to her.

Wren cradled it reverently. "What's this for?"

"Flip it," he said. "If you get heads, you can keep it."

Sending a prayer up to the gods, she flipped and caught it, slapping it on the back of her other hand. The stately profile of Mount Luminis gleamed on the surface. Tails. Trying to still her disappointment, she put the crown back on the desk.

"Bad luck," he said, the corners of his eyes crinkling in a smile. "Eat the cupcake. You'll feel better. In fact, I think I'll have one myself."

She looked at him, unsure of his game. But the cupcake did look good, and she had missed lunch today, what with the bustle of the shop. He was already unwrapping his own, taking a monstrous bite that enveloped half the cupcake in one go. She shrugged and retrieved hers, unwrapping the lace around its base.

The first bite was the best. The sweet vanilla flavor of the fluffy cupcake mingled with the silky sugar of the frosting, hitting her taste buds like a cotton candy cloud. She closed her eyes as she chewed, trying to commit the pleasure of the moment to memory. She opened her eyes and found Kasper watching her with an amused expression on his face.

"Ehts gud," she admitted around the bite of cupcake. Her body buzzed pleasantly as she swallowed.

"Yes, it is," he said, licking frosting off his fingers.

She set the rest of the cupcake on its wrapper on the desk. "It seems a shame to eat it," she said. "It's so pretty. I love making those."

"And your love comes through in every bite," Kasper said. He tossed the coin back to her. "Fancy another go?"

She shrugged and flipped the coin, thinking that this was very unlike how she imagined this meeting would go. When she turned the coin over she laughed with delight. The face of the former King Leon shined up at her. "Heads!"

"I guess your luck has changed," Kasper said, as pleased as she.

Callidus made an exasperated noise against the wall.

"Best two out of three?" Kasper asked.

"No, thank you," she said, clutching the coin in her sweaty palm, dreaming about what she could do with the money. A new dress that wasn't three inches too short. An oil lamp for her room, rather than the stubby candles she had been using. A new palette knife without the wobbly handle of her current model.

"Go ahead," said Kasper. "You can keep the crown even if you lose. Humor me."

Wondering if it was a trap, Wren nevertheless did as she was told, flipping the coin once again.

"Heads!" she said.

"Try again."

Another toss.

"Heads!"

"One more time."

She tossed again.

"Heads," she said, shaking her head in amazement.

"What if I asked you to throw tails," he said.

Getting into it now, she tossed the coin again and hit tails. Not once, but three more times.

"I think you get the point," he said.

She looked at him in amazement. "Is the coin… enchanted?"

"No, my dear. *You* are enchanted."

"What?" She shook her head, confused. "Trust me, I'm about the least lucky person in the city of Maradis."

"You *were* the least lucky person."

"Get to the point, man. I've got places to be," Callidus growled from his place at the bookshelf.

"Don't begrudge me a bit of theatrics," Kasper said. "It's not every day I get to reveal one of our biggest secrets to a new initiate."

Callidus huffed, and Wren looked back and forth between them. She was completely lost now.

Kasper stood and came around the desk, picking up the cupcake and sitting against the desk.

"This cupcake is magic," he said. "It imparts luck upon whoever consumes it."

An incredulous laugh escaped her throat. The man had to be mad. It was the only explanation.

"I assure you, it's no laughing matter. Such an item, in the wrong hands, could change the tide of nations. Wars. Destinies."

"I don't understand," she said. She was overcome with the urge to take her gold crown and get the hell out of this man's office.

"The guilds regulate the practice of their craft within Alesia. But do you truly think that a bunch of chocolatiers or bakers or winemakers warrant this kind of influence?" He waved his hand at the office, at the decadent guildhall around them. "No. This is the secret behind Alesia's political and economic success. The secret behind the royal family. A very special few individuals have an ability. An ability to imbue food with magic. You are one such individual. When you lovingly crafted this cupcake, frosting each rose petal, you filled it with magic. With luck. So that whoever ate it—their life would be forever changed."

Wren's mouth fell open as she looked from the cupcake to Kasper's face. Could it be true? It was insanity. Magic. True, there were tales of magic. Witches and sorcerers and genies in bottles. But they were children's tales. There was no true magic in the world. Just the grim reality of working hard until your body broke down and they laid you in the ground. If there had been anything special or magical about her, her life would have gone very differently up to this point. But she looked down at the golden coin, sitting so mundanely in her hand. She couldn't deny that something strange had happened to that coin.

"It is much to take in at first, I know." Kasper set down the cupcake. "But I assure you, it's all true. And now you understand why we can't have products like this, made by a person like yourself, out in the world."

Wren stilled, her body growing as taut as a wire. Here it was, what some part of her had been expecting all along. Girls like her didn't happen upon magic cupcakes and a fortune in gold. "What do you mean to do with me?" Wren asked, grasping the supple leather arms of her chair. She glanced at Callidus, leaning by the door. Is this why he had stayed? To intercept her when she tried to make a run for it?

"My, you are a skittish thing! I'm sorry, my dear. I didn't mean for that to sound so ominous," Kasper said. "We want to train you. You have a rare gift, and it is valuable to this Guild and the king. Only the highest levels within the Guild know of this secret—the grandmasters of the Guild, like Callidus and myself. You will become one of us."

Words fled as a sliver of hope surfaced within her. She looked around at the room they sat in, at the casual luxuries that she had never dreamed of having. Could he be serious?

"I assure you it will be quite a pleasant life," Kasper said. "We're not all so serious as Callidus. There will be other students for you to learn with, friends to make. Of course, you cannot share the true nature of this secret with them, but that won't be too difficult. What do you say?"

Wren looked between Kasper and Callidus, her thoughts spinning. Though she didn't generally trust people, she had found over the last few years that she had a knack for reading them. Despite Kasper's seemingly calm exterior, lines around his kind eyes betrayed his tension. "I don't have a choice in this, do I?" she asked, realizing the true nature of this summons.

"I'm afraid not, my dear, but it is truly an honor we are bestowing on you. Besides," he said, leaning forward. "Do you have somewhere better to be?"

She thought of the streets of Maradis, the other grubby orphans who had been her family but were now scattered, no doubt dead or selling themselves as whores or mercenaries. She thought of Master Oldrick, refusing to make her a journeyman for four years despite the fact that her skill had surpassed his long ago. It was her turn to sigh. "No," she said. "I don't."

"Excellent!" Kasper clapped his hands and stood, turning to the wooden credenza lining the wall behind his desk. "A toast is in order."

He poured three glasses of what looked like a sweet rosé wine from a crystal decanter. He offered one to Callidus, who declined with a curt shake of his head.

"More for me," Kasper grumbled, handing another glass to Wren. Wren wished she could decline, too, but feared offending the guildmaster. "Stand up, stand up," Kasper said, and she obliged, feeling a sudden poignancy to the moment.

"Now, before we toast to our newest future grandmaster, I need a promise from you. Do you solemnly swear that you will not speak of the truth of your magic, of our magic, to anyone save Callidus, myself, and the others we say are safe?"

"I do," she agreed. She wasn't sure she even believed what he was saying, so there seemed to be little danger in making such a promise.

"Excellent! Cheers!" He clinked his glass to hers and took a healthy swallow. She took a nervous sip of the wine, letting the effervescent flavors of peach and grass swirl across her tongue. She had sampled wine a few times before but hadn't yet developed a palate for it. Watching her father drink himself to death had been enough to quell any burgeoning interest in alcohol.

The instant she swallowed, the wine's sweet finish changed, turning hot and bitter on her tongue.

Callidus strode forward and grabbed the glass from her hand before she could drop it.

Her tongue burned, and when she went to open her mouth, she found she couldn't. It was glued shut. She backed up in panic, knocking into the leather chair, looking from one man to another with wide eyes. She clutched at her throat, grasping fingers leaving red trails down her skin. Had they poisoned her? What was the point of all this show if they were just going to kill her?

"Easy now," Kasper said. "It will pass in a moment, my dear."

He was right. Already the burning sensation was dying, leaving only the tingling aftereffects of the wine and the thudding of her heartbeat in her ears. She opened her mouth wide, gasping in air. "What... What did you do to me?" Her eyes were rimmed with salty tears.

"Standard procedure, my dear. We've found it's best to do it quickly, like pulling out a splinter."

"Do what quickly?"

"You are bound to your oath now. You are physically unable to break your word, to tell our secret. Your secret."

"How?" she croaked, her hands still at her throat, working her jaw as if she could stop it from sealing shut once again. The memory clung to her like taffy.

"Our Guild isn't the only guild with true magic. Vintner's Guild," he said, holding the decanter up to the light. "The magic of truth and lies. Secrets and whispers. Very helpful stuff. In the right hands."

Kasper's pleasant demeanor hadn't changed, but Wren shuddered, eyeing him warily.

Guildmaster Kasper came around the desk and put his arm around her, leading her towards the door. Wren shrank away from his touch, but he didn't seem to notice. "It is a lot to take in, but I promise you will be safe here. A world of wonder is now open to you. Learn. Discover. Explore. And make more cupcakes." He squeezed her shoulder and released her into Callidus's care. "Callidus will see you to Guildmistress Greer, who will take care of getting you situated. I'll come see how you are acclimating tomorrow."

"Thank you," she said haltingly. She felt faint from the whirlwind of the last few minutes and was content to follow Callidus's grim visage into the hallway like an obedient puppy. Kasper said she would be safe here. Dare she believe him? She had learned through trial and painful error what it took to be safe in this world. Blend in. Work hard and don't cause trouble. These things had kept her safe at Master Oldrick's. Would it be enough here?

Callidus towed her back down the corridor towards the staircase. As they reached the landing, a muffled crash sounded behind them, emanating from Guildmaster Kasper's office.

Callidus whirled and darted back down the hallway with startling speed, bursting into the office. The two guards looked at each other and followed suit, spears held before them, surcoats billowing behind.

Unsure of what to do, Wren drifted back down the corridor towards the office, not wanting to intrude but overcome with curiosity. When she reached the open door, she gasped.

Kasper was on the floor, his face an unnatural shade of purple. Foam bubbled from his mouth. His body shook and convulsed as Callidus and the guards tried to hold him down, shouting at each other for antidotes and doctors.

But it was over before it began. Kasper gave a final gurgling breath, convulsed once more, and fell still.

Wren's hands flew to her mouth as bile rose in her throat. Kasper's brown eyes, eyes that had sparkled with life just moments before, now bulged out in a blank stare that transfixed her own.

"He's dead," Callidus said, still on his knees, his head hanging in disbelief.

"Poison," one of the guards announced, standing and wiping his mouth with a shaky hand. "Nasty one." He pointed at the cupcake wrapper forgotten on the desk. "Where did that come from? It didn't pass the security screening."

"I brought it up… But the girl…" Callidus said, his voice ghostly. Then his head whipped around, his eyes locking on Wren with such force that she stumbled back.

"It was her confection," he said, pointing a spindly finger at her. "She must have poisoned it. Arrest her."

ABOUT THE AUTHOR

Claire Luana grew up reading everything she could get her hands on and writing every chance she could. Eventually, adulthood won out, and she turned her writing talents to more scholarly pursuits, going to work as a commercial litigation attorney. While continuing to practice law, Claire decided to return to her roots and try her hand once again at creative writing. She has written and published the Moonburner Cycle and the Confectioner Chronicles and is currently working on several new fantasy series. She lives in Seattle, Washington with her husband and two dogs. In her (little) remaining spare time, she loves to hike, travel, binge-watch CW shows, and of course, fall into a good book.

Connect with Claire Luana online at:
Website & Blog: www.claireluana.com
Facebook: www.facebook.com/claireluana
Twitter: www.twitter.com/clairedeluana
Goodreads:
www.goodreads.com/author/show/15207082.Claire_Luana
Amazon: www.amazon.com/Claire-Luana/e/B01F28F3W4
Instagram: www.instagram.com/claireluana

Check out these other reads by CLAIRE LUANA

The Moonburner Cycle

Moonburner, Book One

Sunburner, Book Two

Starburner, Book Three

Burning Fate, Prequel